The Scarlet Plague
&
The Game

Jack London

The Scarlet Plague & The Game

The present edition is a reproduction of previous publication of this classic work. Minor typographical errors may have been corrected without note, however, for an authentic reading experience the spelling, punctuation, and capitalization have been retained from the original text.

ISBN: 978-1-64799-426-6

CONTENTS

THE SCARLET PLAGUE

THE GAME

THE SCARLET PLAGUE

I

THE way led along upon what had once been the embankment of a railroad. But no train had run upon it for many years. The forest on either side swelled up the slopes of the embankment and crested across it in a green wave of trees and bushes. The trail was as narrow as a man's body, and was no more than a wild-animal runway. Occasionally, a piece of rusty iron, showing through the forest-mould, advertised that the rail and the ties still remained. In one place, a ten-inch tree, bursting through at a connection, had lifted the end of a rail clearly into view. The tie had evidently followed the rail, held to it by the spike long enough for its bed to be filled with gravel and rotten leaves, so that now the crumbling, rotten timber thrust itself up at a curious slant. Old as the road was, it was manifest that it had been of the mono-rail type.

An old man and a boy travelled along this runway. They moved slowly, for the old man was very old, a touch of palsy made his movements tremulous, and he leaned heavily upon his staff. A rude skull-cap of goat-skin protected his head from the sun. From beneath this fell a scant fringe of stained and dirty-white hair. A visor, ingeniously made from a large leaf, shielded his eyes, and from under this he peered at the way of his feet on the trail. His beard, which should have been snow-white but which showed the same weather-wear and camp-stain as his hair, fell nearly to his waist in a great tangled mass. About his chest and shoulders hung a single, mangy garment of goat-skin. His arms and legs, withered and skinny, betokened extreme age, as well as did their sunburn and scars and scratches betoken long years of exposure to the elements.

The boy, who led the way, checking the eagerness of his muscles to the slow progress of the elder, likewise wore a single garment—a ragged-edged piece of bear-skin, with a hole in the middle through which he had thrust his head. He could not have been more than twelve years old. Tucked coquettishly over one ear was the freshly severed tail of a pig. In one hand he carried a medium-sized bow and an arrow.

On his back was a quiverful of arrows. From a sheath hanging about his neck on a thong, projected the battered handle of a hunting knife. He was as brown as a berry, and walked softly, with almost a catlike tread. In marked contrast with his sunburned skin were his eyes—blue, deep blue, but keen and sharp as a pair of gimlets. They seemed to bore into aft about him in a way that was habitual. As he went along he smelled things, as well, his distended, quivering nostrils carrying to his brain an endless series of messages from the outside world. Also, his hearing was acute, and had been so trained that it operated automatically. Without conscious effort, he heard all the slight sounds in the apparent quiet—heard, and differentiated, and classified these sounds—whether they were of the wind rustling the leaves, of the humming of bees and gnats, of the distant rumble of the sea that drifted to him only in lulls, or of the gopher, just under his foot, shoving a pouchful of earth into the entrance of his hole.

Suddenly he became alertly tense. Sound, sight, and odor had given him a simultaneous warning. His hand went back to the old man, touching him, and the pair stood still. Ahead, at one side of the top of the embankment, arose a crackling sound, and the boy's gaze was fixed on the tops of the agitated bushes. Then a large bear, a grizzly, crashed into view, and likewise stopped abruptly, at sight of the humans. He did not like them, and growled querulously. Slowly the boy fitted the arrow to the bow, and slowly he pulled the bowstring taut. But he never removed his eyes from the bear.

The old man peered from under his green leaf at the danger, and stood as quietly as the boy. For a few seconds this mutual scrutinizing went on; then, the bear betraying a growing irritability, the boy, with a movement of his head, indicated that the old man must step aside from the trail and go down the embankment. The boy followed, going backward, still holding the bow taut and ready. They waited till a crashing among the bushes from the opposite side of the embankment told them the bear had gone on. The boy grinned as he led back to the trail.

"A big un, Granser," he chuckled.

The old man shook his head.

"They get thicker every day," he complained in a thin, undependable falsetto. "Who'd have thought I'd live to see the time when a man would be afraid of his life on the way to the Cliff House. When I was a boy, Edwin, men and women and little babies used to come out here from San Francisco by tens of thousands on a nice day. And there weren't any bears then. No, sir. They used to pay money to look at them in cages, they were that rare."

"What is money, Granser?"

Before the old man could answer, the boy recollected and triumphantly shoved his hand into a pouch under his bear-skin and pulled forth a battered and tarnished silver dollar. The old man's eyes glistened, as he held the coin close to them.

"I can't see," he muttered. "You look and see if you can make out the date, Edwin."

The boy laughed.

"You're a great Granser," he cried delightedly, "always making believe them little marks mean something."

The old man manifested an accustomed chagrin as he brought the coin back again close to his own eyes.

"2012," he shrilled, and then fell to cackling grotesquely. "That was the year Morgan the Fifth was appointed President of the United States by the Board of Magnates. It must have been one of the last coins minted, for the Scarlet Death came in 2013. Lord! Lord!—think of it! Sixty years ago, and I am the only person alive to-day that lived in those times. Where did you find it, Edwin?"

The boy, who had been regarding him with the tolerant curiousness one accords to the prattlings of the feeble-minded, answered promptly.

"I got it off of Hoo-Hoo. He found it when we was herdin' goats down near San José last spring. Hoo-Hoo said it was money. Ain't you hungry, Granser?"

The ancient caught his staff in a tighter grip and urged along the trail, his old eyes shining greedily.

"I hope Har-Lip 's found a crab... or two," he mumbled. "They're good eating, crabs, mighty good eating when you've no more teeth and you've got grandsons that love their old grandsire and make a point of catching crabs for him. When I was a boy—"

But Edwin, suddenly stopped by what he saw, was drawing the bowstring on a fitted arrow. He had paused on the brink of a crevasse in the embankment. An ancient culvert had here washed out, and the stream, no longer confined, had cut a passage through the fill. On the opposite side, the end of a rail projected and overhung. It showed rustily through the creeping vines which overran it. Beyond, crouching by a bush, a rabbit looked across at him in trembling hesitancy. Fully fifty feet was the distance, but the arrow flashed true; and the transfixed rabbit, crying out in sudden fright and hurt, struggled painfully away into the brush. The boy himself was a flash of brown skin and flying fur as he bounded down the steep wall of the gap and up the other side. His lean muscles were springs of steel that released into graceful and efficient action. A hundred feet beyond, in a tangle of bushes, he overtook the wounded creature, knocked its head on a convenient tree-trunk, and turned it over to Granser to carry.

"Rabbit is good, very good," the ancient quavered, "but when it comes to a toothsome delicacy I prefer crab. When I was a boy—"

"Why do you say so much that ain't got no sense?" Edwin impatiently interrupted the other's threatened garrulousness.

The boy did not exactly utter these words, but something that remotely resembled them and that was more guttural and explosive and economical of qualifying phrases. His speech showed distant kinship with that of the old man, and the latter's speech was approximately an English that had gone through a bath of corrupt usage.

"What I want to know," Edwin continued, "is why you call crab 'toothsome delicacy'? Crab is crab, ain't it? No one I never heard calls it such funny things."

The old man sighed but did not answer, and they moved on in silence. The surf grew suddenly louder, as they emerged from the forest upon a stretch of sand dunes bordering the sea. A few goats were browsing among the sandy hillocks, and a skin-clad boy, aided by a wolfish-looking dog that was only faintly reminiscent of a collie, was watching them. Mingled with the roar of the surf was a continuous, deep-throated barking or bellowing, which came from a cluster of jagged rocks a hundred yards out from shore. Here huge sea-lions hauled themselves up to lie in the sun or battle with one another. In the immediate foreground arose the smoke of a fire, tended by a third savage-looking boy. Crouched near him were several wolfish dogs similar to the one that guarded the goats.

The old man accelerated his pace, sniffing eagerly as he neared the fire.

"Mussels!" he muttered ecstatically. "Mussels! And ain't that a crab, Hoo-Hoo? Ain't that a crab? My, my, you boys are good to your old grandsire."

Hoo-Hoo, who was apparently of the same age as Edwin, grinned.

"All you want, Granser. I got four."

The old man's palsied eagerness was pitiful. Sitting down in the sand as quickly as his stiff limbs would let him, he poked a large rock-mussel from out of the coals. The heat had forced its shells apart, and the meat, salmon-colored, was thoroughly cooked. Between thumb and forefinger, in trembling haste, he caught the morsel and carried it to his mouth. But it was too hot, and the next moment was violently ejected. The old man spluttered with the pain, and tears ran out of his eyes and down his cheeks.

The boys were true savages, possessing only the cruel humor of the savage. To them the incident was excruciatingly funny, and they burst into loud laughter. Hoo-Hoo danced up and down, while Edwin rolled gleefully on the ground. The boy with the goats came running to join in the fun.

"Set 'em to cool, Edwin, set 'em to cool," the old man besought, in the midst of his grief, making no attempt to wipe away the tears that still flowed from his eyes. "And cool a crab, Edwin, too. You know your grandsire likes crabs."

From the coals arose a great sizzling, which proceeded from the many mussels bursting open their shells and exuding their moisture. They were large shellfish, running from three to six inches in length. The boys raked them out with sticks and placed them on a large piece of driftwood to cool.

"When I was a boy, we did not laugh at our elders; we respected them."

The boys took no notice, and Granser continued to babble an incoherent flow of complaint and censure. But this time he was more careful, and did not burn his mouth. All began to eat, using nothing but their hands and making loud mouth-noises and lip-smackings. The third boy, who was called Hare-Lip, slyly deposited a pinch of sand on a mussel the ancient was carrying to his mouth; and when the grit of it bit into the old fellow's mucous membrane and gums, the laughter was again uproarious. He was unaware that a joke had been played on him, and spluttered and spat until

Edwin, relenting, gave him a gourd of fresh water with which to wash out his mouth.

"Where's them crabs, Hoo-Hoo?" Edwin demanded. "Granser's set upon having a snack."

Again Granser's eyes burned with greediness as a large crab was handed to him. It was a shell with legs and all complete, but the meat had long since departed. With shaky fingers and babblings of anticipation, the old man broke off a leg and found it filled with emptiness.

"The crabs, Hoo-Hoo?" he wailed. "The crabs?"

"I was fooling Granser. They ain't no crabs! I never found one."

The boys were overwhelmed with delight at sight of the tears of senile disappointment that dribbled down the old man's cheeks. Then, unnoticed, Hoo-Hoo replaced the empty shell with a fresh-cooked crab. Already dismembered, from the cracked legs the white meat sent forth a small cloud of savory steam. This attracted the old man's nostrils, and he looked down in amazement.

The change of his mood to one of joy was immediate. He snuffled and muttered and mumbled, making almost a croon of delight, as he began to eat. Of this the boys took little notice, for it was an accustomed spectacle. Nor did they notice his occasional exclamations and utterances of phrases which meant nothing to them, as, for instance, when he smacked his lips and champed his gums while muttering: "Mayonnaise! Just think—mayonnaise! And it's sixty years since the last was ever made! Two generations and never a smell of it! Why, in those days it was served in every restaurant with crab."

When he could eat no more, the old man sighed, wiped his hands on his naked legs, and gazed out over the sea. With the content of a full stomach, he waxed reminiscent.

"To think of it! I've seen this beach alive with men, women, and children on a pleasant Sunday. And there weren't any bears to eat them up, either. And right up there on the cliff was a big restaurant where you could get anything you wanted to eat. Four million people lived in San Francisco then. And now, in the whole city and county there aren't forty all told. And out there on the sea were ships and ships always to be seen, going in for the Golden Gate or coming out. And airships in the air—dirigibles and flying machines. They could travel two hundred miles an hour. The mail contracts with the New York and San Francisco Limited demanded that for the minimum. There was a chap, a Frenchman, I forget his name, who succeeded in making three hundred; but the thing was risky, too risky for conservative persons. But he was on the right clew, and he would have managed it if it hadn't been for the Great Plague. When I was a boy, there were men alive who remembered the coming of the first aeroplanes, and now I have lived to see the last of them, and that sixty years ago."

The old man babbled on, unheeded by the boys, who were long accustomed to his garrulousness, and whose vocabularies, besides, lacked the greater portion of the words he used. It was noticeable that in these rambling soliloquies his English seemed to recrudesce into better construction and phraseology. But when he talked directly with the boys it lapsed, largely, into their own uncouth and simpler forms.

"But there weren't many crabs in those days," the old man wandered on. "They were fished out, and they were great delicacies. The open season was only a month long, too. And now crabs are accessible the whole year around. Think of it—catching all the crabs you want, any time you want, in the surf of the Cliff House beach!"

A sudden commotion among the goats brought the boys to their feet. The dogs about the fire rushed to join their snarling fellow who guarded the goats, while the goats themselves stampeded in the direction of their human protectors. A half dozen forms, lean and gray, glided about on the sand hillocks and faced the bristling dogs. Edwin arched an arrow that fell short. But Hare-Lip, with a sling such as David carried into battle against Goliath, hurled a stone through the air that whistled from the speed of its flight. It fell squarely among the wolves and caused them to slink away toward the dark depths of the eucalyptus forest.

The boys laughed and lay down again in the sand, while Granser sighed ponderously. He had eaten too much, and, with hands clasped on his paunch, the fingers interlaced, he resumed his maunderings.

"'The fleeting systems lapse like foam,'" he mumbled what was evidently a quotation. "That's it—foam, and fleeting. All man's toil upon the planet was just so much foam. He domesticated the serviceable animals, destroyed the hostile ones, and cleared the land of its wild vegetation. And then he passed, and the flood of primordial life rolled back again, sweeping his handiwork away—the weeds and the forest inundated his fields, the beasts of prey swept over his flocks, and now there are wolves on the Cliff House beach." He was appalled by the thought. "Where four million people disported themselves, the wild wolves roam to-day, and the savage progeny of our loins, with prehistoric weapons, defend themselves against the fanged despoilers. Think of it! And all because of the Scarlet Death—"

The adjective had caught Hare-Lip's ear.

"He's always saying that," he said to Edwin. "What is scarlet?"

"'The scarlet of the maples can shake me like the cry of bugles going by,'" the old man quoted.

"It's red," Edwin answered the question. "And you don't know it because you come from the Chauffeur Tribe. They never did know nothing, none of them. Scarlet is red—I know that."

"Red is red, ain't it?" Hare-Lip grumbled. "Then what's the good of gettin' cocky and calling it scarlet?"

"Granser, what for do you always say so much what nobody knows?" he asked. "Scarlet ain't anything, but red is red. Why don't you say red, then?"

"Red is not the right word," was the reply. "The plague was scarlet. The whole face and body turned scarlet in an hour's time. Don't I know? Didn't I see enough of it? And I am telling you it was scarlet because—well, because it was scarlet. There is no other word for it."

"Red is good enough for me," Hare-Lip muttered obstinately. "My dad calls red red, and he ought to know. He says everybody died of the Red Death."

"Your dad is a common fellow, descended from a common fellow," Granser retorted heatedly. "Don't I know the beginnings of the Chauffeurs? Your grandsire was a chauffeur, a servant, and without education. He worked for other persons. But your grandmother was of good stock, only the children did not take after her. Don't I remember when I first met them, catching fish at Lake Temescal?"

"What is education?" Edwin asked.

"Calling red scarlet," Hare-Lip sneered, then returned to the attack on Granser. "My dad told me, an' he got it from his dad afore he croaked, that your wife was a Santa Rosan, an' that she was sure no account. He said she was a hash-slinger before the Red Death, though I don't know what a hash-slinger is. You can tell me, Edwin."

But Edwin shook his head in token of ignorance.

"It is true, she was a waitress," Granser acknowledged. "But she was a good woman, and your mother was her daughter. Women were very scarce in the days after the Plague. She was the only wife I could find, even if she was a hash-slinger, as your father calls it. But it is not nice to talk about our progenitors that way."

"Dad says that the wife of the first Chauffeur was a lady—"

"What's a lady?" Hoo-Hoo demanded.

"A lady 's a Chauffeur squaw," was the quick reply of Hare-Lip.

"The first Chauffeur was Bill, a common fellow, as I said before," the old man expounded; "but his wife was a lady, a great lady. Before the Scarlet Death she was the wife of Van Worden. He was President of the Board of Industrial Magnates, and was one of the dozen men who ruled America. He was worth one billion, eight hundred millions of dollars—coins like you have there in your pouch, Edwin. And then came the Scarlet Death, and his wife became the wife of Bill, the first Chauffeur. He used to beat her, too. I have seen it myself."

Hoo-Hoo, lying on his stomach and idly digging his toes in the sand, cried out and investigated, first, his toe-nail, and next, the small hole he had dug. The other two boys joined him, excavating the sand rapidly with their hands till there lay three skeletons exposed. Two were of adults, the third being that of a part-grown child. The old man hudged along on the ground and peered at the find.

"Plague victims," he announced. "That's the way they died everywhere in the last days. This must have been a family, running away from the contagion and perishing here on the Cliff House beach. They—what are you doing, Edwin?"

This question was asked in sudden dismay, as Edwin, using the back of his hunting knife, began to knock out the teeth from the jaws of one of the skulls.

"Going to string 'em," was the response.

The three boys were now hard at it; and quite a knocking and hammering arose, in which Granser babbled on unnoticed.

"You are true savages. Already has begun the custom of wearing human teeth. In another generation you will be perforating your noses and ears and wearing ornaments of bone and shell. I know. The human race is doomed to sink back farther and farther into the primitive night ere again it begins its bloody climb upward to civilization. When we increase and feel the lack of room, we will proceed to kill one another. And then I suppose you will wear human scalp-locks at your waist, as well—as you, Edwin, who are the gentlest of my grandsons, have already begun with that vile pigtail. Throw it away, Edwin, boy; throw it away."

"What a gabble the old geezer makes," Hare-Lip remarked, when, the teeth all extracted, they began an attempt at equal division.

They were very quick and abrupt in their actions, and their speech, in moments of hot discussion over the allotment of the choicer teeth, was truly a gabble. They spoke in monosyllables and short jerky sentences that was more a gibberish than a language. And yet, through it ran hints of grammatical construction, and appeared vestiges of the conjugation of some superior culture. Even the speech of Granser was so corrupt that were it put down literally it would be almost so much nonsense to the reader. This, however, was when he talked with the boys.

When he got into the full swing of babbling to himself, it slowly purged itself into pure English. The sentences grew longer and were enunciated with a rhythm and ease that was reminiscent of the lecture platform.

"Tell us about the Red Death, Granser," Hare-Lip demanded, when the teeth affair had been satisfactorily concluded.

"The Scarlet Death," Edwin corrected.

"An' don't work all that funny lingo on us," Hare-Lip went on. "Talk sensible, Granser, like a Santa Rosan ought to talk. Other Santa Rosans don't talk like you."

II

THE old man showed pleasure in being thus called upon. He cleared his throat and began.

"Twenty or thirty years ago my story was in great demand. But in these days nobody seems interested—"

"There you go!" Hare-Lip cried hotly. "Cut out the funny stuff and talk sensible. What's interested? You talk like a baby that don't know how."

"Let him alone," Edwin urged, "or he'll get mad and won't talk at all. Skip the funny places. We'll catch on to some of what he tells us."

"Let her go, Granser," Hoo-Hoo encouraged; for the old man was already maundering about the disrespect for elders and the reversion to cruelty of all humans that fell from high culture to primitive conditions.

The tale began.

"There were very many people in the world in those days. San Francisco alone held four millions—"

"What is millions?" Edwin interrupted.

Granser looked at him kindly.

"I know you cannot count beyond ten, so I will tell you. Hold up your two hands. On both of them you have altogether ten fingers and thumbs. Very well. I now take this grain of sand—you hold it,

Hoo-Hoo." He dropped the grain of sand into the lad's palm and went on. "Now that grain of sand stands for the ten fingers of Edwin. I add another grain. That's ten more fingers. And I add another, and another, and another, until I have added as many grains as Edwin has fingers and thumbs. That makes what I call one hundred. Remember that word—one hundred. Now I put this pebble in Hare-Lip's hand. It stands for ten grains of sand, or ten tens of fingers, or one hundred fingers. I put in ten pebbles. They stand for a thousand fingers. I take a mussel-shell, and it stands for ten pebbles, or one hundred grains of sand, or one thousand fingers...." And so on, laboriously, and with much reiteration, he strove to build up in their minds a crude conception of numbers. As the quantities increased, he had the boys holding different magnitudes in each of their hands. For still higher sums, he laid the symbols on the log of driftwood; and for symbols he was hard put, being compelled to use the teeth from the skulls for millions, and the crab-shells for billions. It was here that he stopped, for the boys were showing signs of becoming tired.

"There were four million people in San Francisco—four teeth."

The boys' eyes ranged along from the teeth and from hand to hand, down through the pebbles and sand-grains to Edwin's fingers. And back again they ranged along the ascending series in the effort to grasp such inconceivable numbers.

"That was a lot of folks, Granser," Edwin at last hazarded.

"Like sand on the beach here, like sand on the beach, each grain of sand a man, or woman, or child. Yes, my boy, all those people lived right here in San Francisco. And at one time or another all those people came out on this very beach—more people than there are grains of sand. More—more—more. And San Francisco was a noble city. And across the bay—where we camped last year, even more people lived, clear from Point Richmond, on the level ground and on the hills, all the way around to San Leandro—one great city of seven million people.—Seven teeth... there, that's it, seven millions."

Again the boys' eyes ranged up and down from Edwin's fingers to the teeth on the log.

"The world was full of people. The census of 2010 gave eight billions for the whole world—eight crab-shells, yes, eight billions. It was not like to-day. Mankind knew a great deal more about getting food. And the more food there was, the more people there were. In the year 1800, there were one hundred and seventy millions in Europe alone. One hundred years later—a grain of sand, Hoo-Hoo—one hundred years later, at 1900, there were five hundred millions in Europe—five grains of sand, Hoo-Hoo, and this one tooth. This shows how easy was the getting of food, and how men increased. And in the year 2000 there were fifteen hundred millions in Europe. And it was the same all over the rest of the world. Eight crab-shells there, yes, eight billion people were alive on the earth when the Scarlet Death began.

"I was a young man when the Plague came—twenty-seven years old; and I lived on the other side of San Francisco Bay, in Berkeley. You remember those great stone houses, Edwin, when we came down the hills from Contra Costa? That was where I lived, in those stone houses. I was a professor of English literature."

Much of this was over the heads of the boys, but they strove to comprehend dimly this tale of the past.

"What was them stone houses for?" Hare-Lip queried.

"You remember when your dad taught you to swim?" The boy nodded. "Well, in the University of California—that is the name we had for the houses—we taught young men and women how to think, just as I have taught you now, by sand and pebbles and shells, to know how many people lived in those days. There was very much to teach. The young men and women we taught were called students. We had large rooms in which we taught. I talked to them, forty or fifty at a time, just as I am talking to you now. I told them about the books other men had written before their time, and even, sometimes, in their time—"

"Was that all you did?—just talk, talk, talk?" Hoo-Hoo demanded. "Who hunted your meat for you? and milked the goats? and caught the fish?"

"A sensible question, Hoo-Hoo, a sensible question. As I have told you, in those days food-getting was easy. We were very wise. A few men got the food for many men. The other men did other things. As you say, I talked. I talked all the time, and for this food was given me—much food, fine food, beautiful food, food that I have not tasted in sixty years and shall never taste again. I sometimes think the most wonderful achievement of our tremendous civilization was food—its inconceivable abundance, its infinite variety, its marvellous delicacy. O my grandsons, life was life in those days, when we had such wonderful things to eat."

This was beyond the boys, and they let it slip by, words and thoughts, as a mere senile wandering in the narrative.

"Our food-getters were called freemen. This was a joke. We of the ruling classes owned all the land, all the machines, everything. These food-getters were our slaves. We took almost all the food they got, and left them a little so that they might eat, and work, and get us more food—"

"I'd have gone into the forest and got food for myself," Hare-Lip announced; "and if any man tried to take it away from me, I'd have killed him."

The old man laughed.

"Did I not tell you that we of the ruling class owned all the land, all the forest, everything? Any food-getter who would not get food for us, him we punished or compelled to starve to death. And very few did that. They preferred to get food for us, and make clothes for us, and prepare and administer to us a thousand—a mussel-shell, Hoo-Hoo—a thousand satisfactions and delights. And I was Professor Smith in those days—Professor James Howard Smith. And my lecture courses were very popular—that is, very many of the young men and women liked to hear me talk about the books other men had written.

"And I was very happy, and I had beautiful things to eat. And my hands were soft, because I did no work with them, and my body was clean all over and dressed in the softest garments—

"He surveyed his mangy goat-skin with disgust.

"We did not wear such things in those days. Even the slaves had better garments. And we were most clean. We washed our faces and hands often every day. You boys never wash unless you fall into the water or go swimming."

"Neither do you Granzer," Hoo-Hoo retorted.

"I know, I know, I am a filthy old man, but times have changed.

Nobody washes these days, there are no conveniences. It is sixty years since I have seen a piece of soap.

"You do not know what soap is, and I shall not tell you, for I am telling the story of the Scarlet Death. You know what sickness is. We called it a disease. Very many of the diseases came from what we called germs. Remember that word—germs. A germ is a very small thing. It is like a woodtick, such as you find on the dogs in the spring of the year when they run in the forest. Only the germ is very small. It is so small that you cannot see it—"

Hoo-Hoo began to laugh.

"You're a queer un, Granser, talking about things you can't see. If you can't see 'em, how do you know they are? That's what I want to know. How do you know anything you can't see?"

"A good question, a very good question, Hoo-Hoo. But we did see—some of them. We had what we called microscopes and ultramicroscopes, and we put them to our eyes and looked through them, so that we saw things larger than they really were, and many things we could not see without the microscopes at all. Our best ultramicroscopes could make a germ look forty thousand times larger. A mussel-shell is a thousand fingers like Edwin's. Take forty mussel-shells, and by as many times larger was the germ when we looked at it through a microscope. And after that, we had other ways, by using what we called moving pictures, of making the forty-thousand-times germ many, many thousand times larger still. And thus we saw all these things which our eyes of themselves could not see. Take a grain of sand. Break it into ten pieces. Take one piece and break it into ten. Break one of those pieces into ten, and one of those into ten, and one of those into ten, and one of those into ten, and do it all day, and maybe, by sunset, you will have a piece as small as one of the germs." The boys were openly incredulous. Hare-Lip sniffed and sneered and Hoo-Hoo snickered, until Edwin nudged them to be silent.

"The woodtick sucks the blood of the dog, but the germ, being so very small, goes right into the blood of the body, and there it has many children. In those days there would be as many as a billion—a crab-shell, please—as many as that crab-shell in one man's body. We called germs micro-organisms. When a few million, or a billion, of them were in a man, in all the blood of a man, he was sick. These germs were a disease. There were many different kinds of them—more different kinds than there are grains of sand on this beach. We knew only a few of the kinds. The micro-organic world was an invisible world, a world we could not see, and we knew very little about it. Yet we did know something. There was the bacillus anthracis; there was the micrococcus; there was the Bacterium termo, and the Bacterium lactis—that's what turns the goat milk sour even to this day, Hare-Lip; and there were Schizomycetes without end. And there were many others...."

Here the old man launched into a disquisition on germs and their natures, using words and phrases of such extraordinary length and meaninglessness, that the boys grinned at one another and looked out over the deserted ocean till they forgot the old man was babbling on.

"But the Scarlet Death, Granser," Edwin at last suggested.

Granser recollected himself, and with a start tore himself away from the rostrum of the lecture-hall, where, to another world audience, he had been expounding the latest theory, sixty years gone, of germs and germ-diseases.

"Yes, yes, Edwin; I had forgotten. Sometimes the memory of the past is very strong upon me, and I forget that I am a dirty old man, clad in goat-skin, wandering with my savage grandsons who are goatherds in the primeval wilderness. 'The fleeting systems lapse like foam,' and so lapsed our glorious, colossal civilization. I am Granser, a tired old man. I belong to the tribe of Santa Rosans. I married into that tribe. My sons and daughters married into the Chauffeurs, the Sacramen-tos, and the Palo-Altos. You, Hare-Lip, are of the Chauffeurs. You, Edwin, are of the Sacramentos. And you, Hoo-Hoo, are of the Palo-Altos. Your tribe takes its name from a town that was near the seat of another great institution of learning. It was called Stanford University. Yes, I remember now. It is perfectly clear. I was telling you of the Scarlet Death. Where was I in my story?"

"You was telling about germs, the things you can't see but which make men sick," Edwin prompted.

"Yes, that's where I was. A man did not notice at first when only a few of these germs got into his body. But each germ broke in half and became two germs, and they kept doing this very rapidly so that in a short time there were many millions of them in the body. Then the man was sick. He had a disease, and the disease was named after the kind of a germ that was in him. It might be measles, it might be influenza, it might be yellow fever; it might be any of thousands and thousands of kinds of diseases.

"Now this is the strange thing about these germs. There were always new ones coming to live in men's bodies. Long and long and long ago, when there were only a few men in the world, there were few diseases. But as men increased and lived closely together in great cities and civilizations, new diseases arose, new kinds of germs entered their bodies. Thus were countless millions and billions of human beings killed. And the more thickly men packed together, the more terrible were the new diseases that came to be. Long before my time, in the middle ages, there was the Black Plague that swept across Europe. It swept across Europe many times. There was tuberculosis, that entered into men wherever they were thickly packed. A hundred years before my time there was the bubonic plague. And in Africa was the sleeping sickness. The bacteriologists fought all these sicknesses and destroyed them, just as you boys fight the wolves away from your goats, or squash the mosquitoes that light on you. The bacteriologists—"

"But, Granser, what is a what-you-call-it?" Edwin interrupted.

"You, Edwin, are a goatherd. Your task is to watch the goats. You know a great deal about goats. A bacteriologist watches germs. That's his task, and he knows a great deal about them. So, as I was saying, the bacteriologists fought with the germs and destroyed them—sometimes. There was leprosy, a horrible disease. A hundred years before I was born, the bacteriologists discovered the germ of leprosy. They knew all about it. They made pictures of it. I have seen those pictures. But they never found a way to kill it. But in 1984, there was the Pantoblast Plague, a disease that broke out in a country called Brazil and that killed millions of people. But the bacteriologists found it out, and found the way to kill it, so that the Pantoblast Plague went no farther. They made what they called a serum, which they put into a man's body and which killed the pantoblast germs without killing the man. And in 1910, there was Pellagra, and also the hookworm. These were easily killed by the bacteriologists. But in 1947 there arose a new disease that had never been seen before. It got into the bodies of babies of only ten months old or less, and it made them unable to move their hands and feet, or to eat, or anything; and the bacteriologists were eleven years in discovering how to kill that particular germ and save the babies.

"In spite of all these diseases, and of all the new ones that continued to arise, there were more and more men in the world. This was because it was easy to get food. The easier it was to get food, the more men there were; the more men there were, the more thickly were they packed together on the earth; and the more thickly they were packed, the more new kinds of germs became diseases. There were warnings. Soldervetzsky, as early as 1929, told the bacteriologists that they had no guaranty against some new disease, a thousand times more deadly than any they knew, arising and killing by the hundreds of millions and even by the billion. You see, the micro-organic world remained a mystery to the end. They knew there was such a world, and that from time to time armies of new germs emerged from it to kill men.

"And that was all they knew about it. For all they knew, in that invisible micro-organic world there might be as many different kinds of germs as there are grains of sand on this beach. And also, in that same invisible world it might well be that new kinds of germs came to be. It might be there that life originated—the 'abysmal fecundity,' Soldervetzsky called it, applying the words of other men who had written before him...."

It was at this point that Hare-Lip rose to his feet, an expression of huge contempt on his face.

"Granser," he announced, "you make me sick with your gabble. Why don't you tell about the Red Death? If you ain't going to, say so, an' we'll start back for camp."

The old man looked at him and silently began to cry. The weak tears of age rolled down his cheeks and all the feebleness of his eighty-seven years showed in his grief-stricken countenance.

"Sit down," Edwin counselled soothingly. "Granser's all right. He's just gettin' to the Scarlet Death, ain't you, Granser? He's just goin' to tell us about it right now. Sit down, Hare-Lip. Go ahead, Granser."

III

THE old man wiped the tears away on his grimy knuckles and took up the tale in a tremulous, piping voice that soon strengthened as he got the swing of the narrative.

"It was in the summer of 2013 that the Plague came. I was twenty-seven years old, and well do I remember it. Wireless despatches—"

Hare-Lip spat loudly his disgust, and Granser hastened to make amends.

"We talked through the air in those days, thousands and thousands of miles. And the word came of a strange disease that had broken out in New York. There were seventeen millions of people living then in that noblest city of America. Nobody thought anything about the news. It was only a small thing. There had been only a few deaths. It seemed, though, that they had died very quickly, and that one of the first signs of the disease was the turning red of the face and all the body. Within twenty-four hours came the report of the first case in Chicago. And on the same day, it was made public that London, the greatest city in the world, next to Chicago, had been secretly fighting the plague for two weeks and censoring the news despatches—that is, not permitting the word to go forth to the rest of the world that London had the plague.

"It looked serious, but we in California, like everywhere else, were not alarmed. We were sure that the bacteriologists would find a way to overcome this new germ, just as they had overcome other germs in the past. But the trouble was the astonishing quickness with which this germ destroyed human beings, and the fact that it inevitably killed any human body it entered. No one ever recovered. There was the old Asiatic cholera, when you might eat dinner with a well man in the evening, and the next morning, if you got up early enough, you would see him being hauled by your window in the death-cart. But this new plague was quicker than that—much quicker.

"From the moment of the first signs of it, a man would be dead in an hour. Some lasted for several hours. Many died within ten or fifteen minutes of the appearance of the first signs.

"The heart began to beat faster and the heat of the body to increase. Then came the scarlet rash, spreading like wildfire over the face and body. Most persons never noticed the increase in heat and heart-beat, and the first they knew was when the scarlet rash came out. Usually, they had convulsions at the time of the appearance of the rash. But these convulsions did not last long and were not very severe. If one lived through them, he became perfectly quiet, and only did he feel a numbness swiftly creeping up his body from the feet. The heels became numb first, then the legs, and hips, and when the numbness reached as high as his heart he died. They did not rave or sleep. Their minds always remained cool and calm up to the moment their heart numbed and stopped. And another strange thing was the rapidity of decomposition. No sooner was a person dead than the body seemed to fall to pieces, to fly apart, to melt away even as you looked at it. That was one of the reasons the plague spread so rapidly. All the billions of germs in a corpse were so immediately released.

"And it was because of all this that the bacteriologists had so little chance in fighting the germs. They were killed in their laboratories even as they studied the germ of the Scarlet Death. They were heroes. As fast as they perished, others stepped forth and took their places. It was in London that they first isolated it. The news was telegraphed everywhere. Trask was the name of the man who succeeded in this, but within thirty hours he was dead. Then came the struggle in all the laboratories to find something that would kill the plague germs. All drugs failed. You see, the problem was to get a drug, or serum, that would kill the germs in the body and not kill the body. They tried to fight it with other germs, to put into the body of a sick man germs that were the enemies of the plague germs—"

"And you can't see these germ-things, Granser," Hare-Lip objected, "and here you gabble, gabble, gabble about them as if they was anything, when they're nothing at all. Anything you can't see, ain't, that's what. Fighting things that ain't with things that ain't! They must have been all fools in them days. That's why they croaked. I ain't goin' to believe in such rot, I tell you that."

Granser promptly began to weep, while Edwin hotly took up his defence.

"Look here, Hare-Lip, you believe in lots of things you can't see."

Hare-Lip shook his head.

"You believe in dead men walking about. You never seen one dead man walk about."

"I tell you I seen 'em, last winter, when I was wolf-hunting with dad."

"Well, you always spit when you cross running water," Edwin challenged.

"That's to keep off bad luck," was Hare-Lip's defence.

"You believe in bad luck?"

"Sure."

"An' you ain't never seen bad luck," Edwin concluded triumphantly. "You're just as bad as Granser and his germs. You believe in what you don't see. Go on, Granser."

Hare-Lip, crushed by this metaphysical defeat, remained silent, and the old man went on. Often and often, though this narrative must not be clogged by the details, was Granser's tale interrupted while the boys squabbled among themselves. Also, among themselves they kept up a constant, low-voiced exchange of explanation and conjecture, as they strove to follow the old man into his unknown and vanished world.

"The Scarlet Death broke out in San Francisco. The first death came on a Monday morning. By Thursday they were dying like flies in Oakland and San Francisco. They died everywhere—in their beds, at their work, walking along the street. It was on Tuesday that I saw my first death—Miss Collbran, one of my students, sitting right there before my eyes, in my lecture-room. I noticed her face while I was talking. It had suddenly turned scarlet. I ceased speaking and could only look at her, for the first fear of the plague was already on all of us and we knew that it had come. The young women screamed and ran out of the room. So did the young men run out, all but two. Miss Collbran's convulsions were very mild and lasted less than a minute. One of the young men fetched her a glass of water. She drank only a little of it, and cried out:

"'My feet! All sensation has left them.'

"After a minute she said, 'I have no feet. I am unaware that I have any feet. And my knees are cold. I can scarcely feel that I have knees.'

"She lay on the floor, a bundle of notebooks under her head. And we could do nothing. The coldness and the numbness crept up past her hips to her heart, and when it reached her heart she was dead. In fifteen minutes, by the clock—I timed it—she was dead, there, in my own classroom, dead. And she was a very beautiful, strong, healthy young woman. And from the first sign of the plague to her death only fifteen minutes elapsed. That will show you how swift was the Scarlet Death.

"Yet in those few minutes I remained with the dying woman in my classroom, the alarm had spread over the university; and the students, by thousands, all of them, had deserted the lecture-room and laboratories. When I emerged, on my way to make report to the President of the Faculty, I found the university deserted. Across the campus were several stragglers hurrying for their homes. Two of them were running.

"President Hoag, I found in his office, all alone, looking very old and very gray, with a multitude of wrinkles in his face that I had never seen before. At the sight of me, he pulled himself to his feet and tottered away to the inner office, banging the door after him and locking it. You see, he knew I had been exposed, and he was afraid. He shouted to me through the door to go away. I shall never forget my feelings as I walked down the silent corridors and out across that deserted campus. I was not afraid. I had been exposed, and I looked upon myself as already dead. It was not that, but a feeling of awful depression that impressed me. Everything had stopped. It was like the end of the world to me—my world. I had been born within sight and sound of the university. It had been my predestined career. My father had been a professor there before me, and his father before him. For a century and a half had this university, like a splendid machine, been running steadily on. And now, in an instant, it had stopped. It was like seeing the sacred flame die down on some thrice-sacred altar. I was shocked, unutterably shocked.

"When I arrived home, my housekeeper screamed as I entered, and fled away. And when I rang, I found the housemaid had likewise fled. I investigated. In the kitchen I found the cook on the point of departure. But she screamed, too, and in her haste dropped a suitcase of her personal belongings and ran out of the house and across the grounds, still screaming. I can hear her scream to this day. You see, we did not act in this way when ordinary diseases smote us. We were always calm over such things, and sent for the doctors and nurses who knew just what to do. But this was different. It struck so suddenly, and killed so swiftly, and never missed a stroke. When the scarlet rash appeared on a person's face, that person was marked by death. There was never a known case of a recovery.

"I was alone in my big house. As I have told you often before, in those days we could talk with one another over wires or through the air. The telephone bell rang, and I found my brother talking to me. He told me that he was not coming home for fear of catching the plague from me, and that he had taken our two sisters to stop at Professor Bacon's home. He advised me to remain where I was, and wait to find out whether or not I had caught the plague.

"To all of this I agreed, staying in my house and for the first time in my life attempting to cook. And the plague did not come out on me. By means of the telephone I could talk with whomsoever I pleased and get the news. Also, there were the newspapers, and I ordered all of them to be thrown up to my door so that I could know what was happening with the rest of the world.

"New York City and Chicago were in chaos. And what happened with them was happening in all the large cities. A third of the New York police were dead. Their chief was also dead, likewise the mayor. All law and order had ceased. The bodies were lying in the streets un-buried. All railroads and vessels carrying food and such things into the great city had ceased runnings and mobs of the hungry poor were pillaging the stores and warehouses. Murder and robbery and drunkenness were everywhere. Already the people had fled from the city by millions—at first the rich, in their private motor-cars and dirigibles, and then the great mass of the population, on foot, carrying the plague with them, themselves starving and pillaging the farmers and all the towns and villages on the way.

"The man who sent this news, the wireless operator, was alone with his instrument on the top of a lofty building. The people remaining in the city—he estimated them at several hundred thousand—had gone mad from fear and drink, and on all sides of him great fires were raging. He was a hero, that man who staid by his post—an obscure newspaperman, most likely.

"For twenty-four hours, he said, no transatlantic airships had arrived, and no more messages were coming from England. He did state, though, that a message from Berlin—that's in Germany—announced that Hoffmeyer, a bacteriologist of the Metchnikoff School, had discovered the serum for the plague. That was the last word, to this day, that we of America ever received from Europe. If Hoffmeyer discovered the serum, it was too late, or otherwise, long ere this, explorers from Europe would have come looking for us. We can only conclude that what happened in America happened in Europe, and that, at the best, some several score may have survived the Scarlet Death on that whole continent.

"For one day longer the despatches continued to come from New York. Then they, too, ceased. The man who had sent them, perched in his lofty building, had either died of the plague or been consumed in the great conflagrations he had described as raging around him. And what had occurred in New York had been duplicated in all the other cities. It was the same in San Francisco, and Oakland, and Berkeley. By Thursday the people were dying so rapidly that their corpses could not be handled, and dead bodies lay everywhere. Thursday night the panic outrush for the country began. Imagine, my grandsons, people, thicker than the salmon-run you have seen on the Sacramento river, pouring out of the cities by millions, madly over the country, in vain attempt to escape the ubiquitous death. You see, they carried the germs with them. Even the airships of the rich, fleeing for mountain and desert fastnesses, carried the germs.

"Hundreds of these airships escaped to Hawaii, and not only did they bring the plague with them, but they found the plague already there before them. This we learned, by the despatches, until all order in San Francisco vanished, and there were no operators left at their posts to receive or send. It was amazing, astounding, this loss of communication with the world. It was exactly as if the world had ceased, been blotted out. For sixty years that world has no longer existed for me. I know there must be such places as New York, Europe, Asia, and Africa; but not one word has been heard of them—not in sixty years. With the coming of the Scarlet Death the world fell apart, absolutely, irretrievably. Ten thousand years of culture and civilization passed in the twinkling of an eye, 'lapsed like foam.'

"I was telling about the airships of the rich. They carried the plague with them and no matter where they fled, they died. I never encountered but one survivor of any of them—Mungerson. He was afterwards a Santa Rosan, and he married my eldest daughter. He came into the tribe eight years after the plague. He was then nineteen years old, and he was compelled to wait twelve years more before he could marry. You see, there were no unmarried women, and some of the older daughters of the Santa Rosans were already bespoken. So he was forced to wait until my Mary had grown to sixteen years. It was his son, Gimp-Leg, who was killed last year by the mountain lion.

"Mungerson was eleven years old at the time of the plague. His father was one of the Industrial Magnates, a very wealthy, powerful man. It was on his airship, the Condor, that they were fleeing, with all the family, for the wilds of British Columbia, which is far to the north of here. But there was some accident, and they were wrecked near Mount Shasta. You have heard of that mountain. It is far to the north. The plague broke out amongst them, and this boy of eleven was the only survivor. For eight years he was alone, wandering over a deserted land and looking vainly for his own kind. And at last, travelling south, he picked up with us, the Santa Rosans.

"But I am ahead of my story. When the great exodus from the cities around San Francisco Bay began, and while the telephones were still working, I talked with my brother. I told him this flight from the cities was insanity, that there were no symptoms of the plague in me, and that the thing for us to do was to isolate ourselves and our relatives in some safe place. We decided on the Chemistry

Building, at the university, and we planned to lay in a supply of provisions, and by force of arms to prevent any other persons from forcing their presence upon us after we had retired to our refuge.

"All this being arranged, my brother begged me to stay in my own house for at least twenty-four hours more, on the chance of the plague developing in me. To this I agreed, and he promised to come for me next day. We talked on over the details of the provisioning and the defending of the Chemistry Building until the telephone died. It died in the midst of our conversation. That evening there were no electric lights, and I was alone in my house in the darkness. No more newspapers were being printed, so I had no knowledge of what was taking place outside.

"I heard sounds of rioting and of pistol shots, and from my windows I could see the glare of the sky of some conflagration in the direction of Oakland. It was a night of terror. I did not sleep a wink. A man—why and how I do not know—was killed on the sidewalk in front of the house. I heard the rapid reports of an automatic pistol, and a few minutes later the wounded wretch crawled up to my door, moaning and crying out for help. Arming myself with two automatics, I went to him. By the light of a match I ascertained that while he was dying of the bullet wounds, at the same time the plague was on him. I fled indoors, whence I heard him moan and cry out for half an hour longer.

"In the morning, my brother came to me. I had gathered into a handbag what things of value I purposed taking, but when I saw his face I knew that he would never accompany me to the Chemistry Building. The plague was on him. He intended shaking my hand, but I went back hurriedly before him.

"'Look at yourself in the mirror,' I commanded.

"He did so, and at sight of his scarlet face, the color deepening as he looked at it, he sank down nervelessly in a chair.

"'My God!' he said. 'I've got it. Don't come near me. I am a dead man.'

"Then the convulsions seized him. He was two hours in dying, and he was conscious to the last, complaining about the coldness and loss of sensation in his feet, his calves, his thighs, until at last it was his heart and he was dead.

"That was the way the Scarlet Death slew. I caught up my handbag and fled. The sights in the streets were terrible. One stumbled on bodies everywhere. Some were not yet dead. And even as you looked, you saw men sink down with the death fastened upon them. There were numerous fires burning in Berkeley, while Oakland and San Francisco were apparently being swept by vast conflagrations. The smoke of the burning filled the heavens, so that the midday was as a gloomy twilight, and, in the shifts of wind, sometimes the sun shone through dimly, a dull red orb. Truly, my grandsons, it was like the last days of the end of the world.

"There were numerous stalled motor cars, showing that the gasoline and the engine supplies of the garages had given out. I remember one such car. A man and a woman lay back dead in the seats, and on the pavement near it were two more women and a child. Strange and terrible sights there were on every hand. People slipped by silently, furtively, like ghosts—white-faced women carrying infants in their arms; fathers leading children by the hand; singly, and in couples, and in families—all fleeing out of the city of death. Some carried supplies of food, others blankets and valuables, and there were many who carried nothing.

"There was a grocery store—a place where food was sold. The man to whom it belonged—I knew him well—a quiet, sober, but stupid and obstinate fellow, was defending it. The windows and doors had been broken in, but he, inside, hiding behind a counter, was discharging his pistol at a number of men on the sidewalk who were breaking in. In the entrance were several bodies—of men, I decided, whom he had killed earlier in the day. Even as I looked on from a distance, I saw one of the robbers break the windows of the adjoining store, a place where shoes were sold, and deliberately set fire to it. I did not go to the groceryman's assistance. The time for such acts had already passed. Civilization was crumbling, and it was each for himself."

IV

I WENT away hastily, down a cross-street, and at the first corner I saw another tragedy. Two men of the working class had caught a man and a woman with two children, and were robbing them. I knew the man by sight, though I had never been introduced to him. He was a poet whose verses I had long admired. Yet I did not go to his help, for at the moment I came upon the scene there was a pistol shot, and I saw him sinking to the ground. The woman screamed, and she was felled with a fist-blow by one of the brutes. I cried out threateningly, whereupon they discharged their pistols at me and I ran away around the corner. Here I was blocked by an advancing conflagration. The buildings on both sides were burning, and the street was filled with smoke and flame. From somewhere in that murk came a woman's voice calling shrilly for help. But I did not go to her. A man's heart turned to iron amid such scenes, and one heard all too many appeals for help.

"Returning to the corner, I found the two robbers were gone. The poet and his wife lay dead on the pavement. It was a shocking sight. The two children had vanished—whither I could not tell. And I knew, now, why it was that the fleeing persons I encountered slipped along so furtively and with such white faces. In the midst of our civilization, down in our slums and labor-ghettos, we had bred a race of barbarians, of savages; and now, in the time of our calamity, they turned upon us like the wild beasts they were and destroyed us. And they destroyed themselves as well.

"They inflamed themselves with strong drink and committed a thousand atrocities, quarreling and killing one another in the general madness. One group of workingmen I saw, of the better sort, who had banded together, and, with their women and children in their midst, the sick and aged in litters and being carried, and with a number of horses pulling a truck-load of provisions, they were fighting their way out of the city. They made a fine spectacle as they came down the street through the drifting smoke, though they nearly shot me when I first appeared in their path. As they went by, one of their leaders shouted out to me in apologetic explanation. He said they were killing the robbers and looters on sight, and that they had thus banded together as the only-means by which to escape the prowlers.

"It was here that I saw for the first time what I was soon to see so often. One of the marching men had suddenly shown the unmistakable mark of the plague. Immediately those about him drew away, and he, without a remonstrance, stepped out of his place to let them pass on. A woman, most probably his wife, attempted to follow him. She was leading a little boy by the hand. But the husband commanded her sternly to go on, while others laid hands on her and restrained her from following him. This I saw, and I saw the man also, with his scarlet blaze of face, step into a doorway on the opposite side of the street. I heard the report of his pistol, and saw him sink lifeless to the ground.

"After being turned aside twice again by advancing fires, I succeeded in getting through to the university. On the edge of the campus I came upon a party of university folk who were going in the direction of the Chemistry Building. They were all family men, and their families were with them, including the nurses and the servants. Professor Badminton greeted me, I had difficulty in recognizing him. Somewhere he had gone through flames, and his beard was singed off. About his head was a bloody bandage, and his clothes were filthy.

"He told me he had prowlers, and that his brother had been killed the previous night, in the defence of their dwelling.

"Midway across the campus, he pointed suddenly to Mrs. Swinton's face. The unmistakable scarlet was there. Immediately all the other women set up a screaming and began to run away from her. Her two children were with a nurse, and these also ran with the women. But her husband, Doctor Swinton, remained with her.

"'Go on, Smith,' he told me. 'Keep an eye on the children. As for me, I shall stay with my wife. I know she is as already dead, but I can't leave her. Afterwards, if I escape, I shall come to the Chemistry Building, and do you watch for me and let me in.'

"I left him bending over his wife and soothing her last moments, while I ran to overtake the party. We were the last to be admitted to the Chemistry Building. After that, with our automatic rifles we maintained our isolation. By our plans, we had arranged for a company of sixty to be in this refuge. Instead, every one of the number originally planned had added relatives and friends and whole families until there were over four hundred souls. But the Chemistry Building was large, and, standing by itself, was in no danger of being burned by the great fires that raged everywhere in the city.

"A large quantity of provisions had been gathered, and a food committee took charge of it, issuing rations daily to the various families and groups that arranged themselves into messes. A number of committees were appointed, and we developed a very efficient organization. I was on the committee of defence, though for the first day no prowlers came near. We could see them in the distance, however, and by the smoke of their fires knew that several camps of them were occupying the far edge of the campus. Drunkenness was rife, and often we heard them singing ribald songs or insanely shouting. While the world crashed to ruin about them and all the air was filled with the smoke of its burning, these low creatures gave rein to their bestiality and fought and drank and died. And after all, what did it matter? Everybody died anyway, the good and the bad, the efficients and the weaklings, those that loved to live and those that scorned to live. They passed. Everything passed.

"When twenty-four hours had gone by and no signs of the plague were apparent, we congratulated ourselves and set about digging a well. You have seen the great iron pipes which in those days carried water to all the city-dwellers. We feared that the fires in the city would burst the pipes and empty the reservoirs. So we tore up the cement floor of the central court of the Chemistry Building and dug a well. There were many young men, undergraduates, with us, and we worked night and day on the well. And our fears were confirmed. Three hours before we reached water, the pipes went dry.

"A second twenty-four hours passed, and still the plague did not appear among us. We thought we were saved. But we did not know what I afterwards decided to be true, namely, that the period of the incubation of the plague germs in a human's body was a matter of a number of days. It slew so swiftly when once it manifested itself, that we were led to believe that the period of incubation was equally swift. So, when two days had left us unscathed, we were elated with the idea that we were free of the contagion.

"But the third day disillusioned us. I can never forget the night preceding it. I had charge of the night guards from eight to twelve, and from the roof of the building I watched the passing of all man's glorious works. So terrible were the local conflagrations that all the sky was lighted up. One could read the finest print in the red glare. All the world seemed wrapped in flames. San Francisco spouted smoke and fire from a score of vast conflagrations that were like so many active volcanoes. Oakland, San Leandro, Haywards—all were burning; and to the northward, clear to Point Richmond, other fires were at work. It was an awe-inspiring spectacle. Civilization, my grandsons, civilization was passing in a sheet of flame and a breath of death. At ten o'clock that night, the great powder magazines at Point Pinole exploded in rapid succession. So terrific were the concussions that the strong building rocked as in an earthquake, while every pane of glass was broken. It was then that I left the roof and went down the long corridors, from room to room, quieting the alarmed women and telling them what had happened.

"An hour later, at a window on the ground floor, I heard pandemonium break out in the camps of the prowlers. There were cries and screams, and shots from many pistols. As we afterward conjectured, this fight had been precipitated by an attempt on the part of those that were well to drive out those that were sick. At any rate, a number of the plague-stricken prowlers escaped across the campus and drifted against our doors. We warned them back, but they cursed us and discharged a fusillade from their pistols. Professor Merryweather, at one of the windows, was instantly killed, the bullet striking him squarely between the eyes. We opened fire in turn, and all the prowlers fled away with the exception of three. One was a woman. The plague was on them and they were reckless. Like foul fiends, there in the red glare from the skies, with faces blazing, they continued to curse us and fire at us.

One of the men I shot with my own hand. After that the other man and the woman, still cursing us, lay down under our windows, where we were compelled to watch them die of the plague.

"The situation was critical. The explosions of the powder magazines had broken all the windows of the Chemistry Building, so that we were exposed to the germs from the corpses. The sanitary committee was called upon to act, and it responded nobly. Two men were required to go out and remove the corpses, and this meant the probable sacrifice of their own lives, for, having performed the task, they were not to be permitted to reenter the building. One of the professors, who was a bachelor, and one of the undergraduates volunteered. They bade good-bye to us and went forth. They were heroes. They gave up their lives that four hundred others might live. After they had performed their work, they stood for a moment, at a distance, looking at us wistfully. Then they waved their hands in farewell and went away slowly across the campus toward the burning city.

"And yet it was all useless. The next morning the first one of us was smitten with the plague—a little nurse-girl in the family of Professor Stout. It was no time for weak-kneed, sentimental policies. On the chance that she might be the only one, we thrust her forth from the building and commanded her to be gone.

"She went away slowly across the campus, wringing her hands and crying pitifully. We felt like brutes, but what were we to do? There were four hundred of us, and individuals had to be sacrificed.

"In one of the laboratories three families had domiciled themselves, and that afternoon we found among them no less than four corpses and seven cases of the plague in all its different stages.

"Then it was that the horror began. Leaving the dead lie, we forced the living ones to segregate themselves in another room. The plague began to break out among the rest of us, and as fast as the symptoms appeared, we sent the stricken ones to these segregated rooms. We compelled them to walk there by themselves, so as to avoid laying hands on them. It was heartrending. But still the plague raged among us, and room after room was filled with the dead and dying. And so we who were yet clean retreated to the next floor and to the next, before this sea of the dead, that, room by room and floor by floor, inundated the building.

"The place became a charnel house, and in the middle of the night the survivors fled forth, taking nothing with them except arms and ammunition and a heavy store of tinned foods. We camped on the opposite side of the campus from the prowlers, and, while some stood guard, others of us volunteered to scout into the city in quest of horses, motor cars, carts, and wagons, or anything that would carry our provisions and enable us to emulate the banded workingmen I had seen fighting their way out to the open country.

"I was one of these scouts; and Doctor Hoyle, remembering that his motor car had been left behind in his home garage, told me to look for it. We scouted in pairs, and Dombey, a young undergraduate, accompanied me. We had to cross half a mile of the residence portion of the city to get to Doctor Hoyle's home. Here the buildings stood apart, in the midst of trees and grassy lawns, and here the fires had played freaks, burning whole blocks, skipping blocks and often skipping a single house in a block. And here, too, the prowlers were still at their work. We carried our automatic pistols openly in our hands, and looked desperate enough, forsooth, to keep them from attacking us. But at Doctor Hoyle's house the thing happened. Untouched by fire, even as we came to it the smoke of flames burst forth.

"The miscreant who had set fire to it staggered down the steps and out along the driveway. Sticking out of his coat pockets were bottles of whiskey, and he was very drunk. My first impulse was to shoot him, and I have never ceased regretting that I did not. Staggering and maundering to himself, with bloodshot eyes, and a raw and bleeding slash down one side of his bewhiskered face, he was altogether the most nauseating specimen of degradation and filth I had ever encountered. I did not shoot him, and he leaned against a tree on the lawn to let us go by. It was the most absolute, wanton act. Just as we were opposite him, he suddenly drew a pistol and shot Dombey through the head. The next instant I shot him. But it was too late. Dombey expired without a groan, immediately. I doubt if he even knew what had happened to him.

"Leaving the two corpses, I hurried on past the burning house to the garage, and there found Doctor Hoyle's motor car. The tanks were filled with gasoline, and it was ready for use. And it was in this car that I threaded the streets of the ruined city and came back to the survivors on the campus. The other scouts returned, but none had been so fortunate. Professor Fairmead had found a Shetland pony, but the poor creature, tied in a stable and abandoned for days, was so weak from want of food and water that it could carry no burden at all. Some of the men were for turning it loose, but I insisted that we should lead it along with us, so that, if we got out of food, we would have it to eat.

"There were forty-seven of us when we started, many being women and children. The President of the Faculty, an old man to begin with, and now hopelessly broken by the awful happenings of the past week, rode in the motor car with several young children and the aged mother of Professor Fairmead. Wathope, a young professor of English, who had a grievous bullet-wound in his leg, drove the car. The rest of us walked, Professor Fairmead leading the pony.

"It was what should have been a bright summer day, but the smoke from the burning world filled the sky, through which the sun shone murkily, a dull and lifeless orb, blood-red and ominous. But we had grown accustomed to that blood-red sun. With the smoke it was different. It bit into our nostrils and eyes, and there was not one of us whose eyes were not bloodshot. We directed our course to the southeast through the endless miles of suburban residences, travelling along where the first swells of low hills rose from the flat of the central city. It was by this way, only, that we could expect to gain the country.

"Our progress was painfully slow. The women and children could not walk fast. They did not dream of walking, my grandsons, in the way all people walk to-day. In truth, none of us knew how to walk. It was not until after the plague that I learned really to walk. So it was that the pace of the slowest was the pace of all, for we dared not separate on account of the prowlers. There were not so many now of these human beasts of prey. The plague had already well diminished their numbers, but enough still lived to be a constant menace to us. Many of the beautiful residences were untouched by fire, yet smoking ruins were everywhere. The prowlers, too, seemed to have got over their insensate desire to burn, and it was more rarely that we saw houses freshly on fire.

"Several of us scouted among the private garages in search of motor cars and gasoline. But in this we were unsuccessful. The first great flights from the cities had swept all such utilities away. Calgan, a fine young man, was lost in this work. He was shot by prowlers while crossing a lawn. Yet this was our only casualty, though, once, a drunken brute deliberately opened fire on all of us. Luckily, he fired wildly, and we shot him before he had done any hurt.

"At Fruitvale, still in the heart of the magnificent residence section of the city, the plague again smote us. Professor Fair-mead was the victim. Making signs to us that his mother was not to know, he turned aside into the grounds of a beautiful mansion. He sat down forlornly on the steps of the front veranda, and I, having lingered, waved him a last farewell. That night, several miles beyond Fruitvale and still in the city, we made camp. And that night we shifted camp twice to get away from our dead. In the morning there were thirty of us. I shall never forget the President of the Faculty. During the morning's march his wife, who was walking, betrayed the fatal symptoms, and when she drew aside to let us go on, he insisted on leaving the motor car and remaining with her. There was quite a discussion about this, but in the end we gave in. It was just as well, for we knew not which ones of us, if any, might ultimately escape.

"That night, the second of our march, we camped beyond Haywards in the first stretches of country. And in the morning there were eleven of us that lived. Also, during the night, Wathope, the professor with the wounded leg, deserted us in the motor car. He took with him his sister and his mother and most of our tinned provisions. It was that day, in the afternoon, while resting by the wayside, that I saw the last airship I shall ever see. The smoke was much thinner here in the country, and I first sighted the ship drifting and veering helplessly at an elevation of two thousand feet. What had happened I could not conjecture, but even as we looked we saw her bow dip down lower and lower. Then the bulkheads of the various gas-chambers must have burst, for, quite perpendicular, she fell like a plummet to the earth.

"And from that day to this I have not seen another airship. Often and often, during the next few years, I scanned the sky for them, hoping against hope that somewhere in the world civilization had survived. But it was not to be. What happened with us in California must have happened with everybody everywhere.

"Another day, and at Niles there were three of us. Beyond Niles, in the middle of the highway, we found Wathope. The motor car had broken down, and there, on the rugs which they had spread on the ground, lay the bodies of his sister, his mother, and himself.

"Wearied by the unusual exercise of continual walking, that night I slept heavily. In the morning I was alone in the world. Canfield and Parsons, my last companions, were dead of the plague. Of the four hundred that sought shelter in the Chemistry Building, and of the forty-seven that began the march, I alone remained—I and the Shetland pony. Why this should be so there is no explaining. I did not catch the plague, that is all. I was immune. I was merely the one lucky man in a million—just as every survivor was one in a million, or, rather, in several millions, for the proportion was at least that."

V

"FOR two days I sheltered in a pleasant grove where there had been no deaths. In those two days, while badly depressed and believing that my turn would come at any moment, nevertheless I rested and recuperated. So did the pony. And on the third day, putting what small store of tinned provisions I possessed on the pony's back, I started on across a very lonely land. Not a live man, woman, or child, did I encounter, though the dead were everywhere. Food, however, was abundant. The land then was not as it is now. It was all cleared of trees and brush, and it was cultivated. The food for millions of mouths was growing, ripening, and going to waste. From the fields and orchards I gathered vegetables, fruits, and berries. Around the deserted farmhouses I got eggs and caught chickens. And frequently I found supplies of tinned provisions in the store-rooms.

"A strange thing was what was taking place with all the domestic animals. Everywhere they were going wild and preying on one another. The chickens and ducks were the first to be destroyed, while the pigs were the first to go wild, followed by the cats. Nor were the dogs long in adapting themselves to the changed conditions. There was a veritable plague of dogs. They devoured the corpses, barked and howled during the nights, and in the daytime slunk about in the distance. As the time went by, I noticed a change in their behavior. At first they were apart from one another, very suspicious and very prone to fight. But after a not very long while they began to come together and run in packs. The dog, you see, always was a social animal, and this was true before ever he came to be domesticated by man. In the last days of the world before the plague, there were many many very different kinds of dogs—dogs without hair and dogs with warm fur, dogs so small that they would make scarcely a mouthful for other dogs that were as large as mountain lions. Well, all the small dogs, and the weak types, were killed by their fellows. Also, the very large ones were not adapted for the wild life and bred out. As a result, the many different kinds of dogs disappeared, and there remained, running in packs, the medium-sized wolfish dogs that you know to-day."

"But the cats don't run in packs, Granser," Hoo-Hoo objected.

"The cat was never a social animal. As one writer in the nineteenth century said, the cat walks by himself. He always walked by himself, from before the time he was tamed by man, down through the long ages of domestication, to to-day when once more he is wild.

"The horses also went wild, and all the fine breeds we had degenerated into the small mustang horse you know to-day. The cows likewise went wild, as did the pigeons and the sheep. And that a few of the chickens survived you know yourself. But the wild chicken of to-day is quite a different thing from the chickens we had in those days.

"But I must go on with my story. I travelled through a deserted land. As the time went by I began to yearn more and more for human beings. But I never found one, and I grew lonelier and lonelier. I crossed Livermore Valley and the mountains between it and the great valley of the San Joaquin. You have never seen that valley, but it is very large and it is the home of the wild horse. There are great droves there, thousands and tens of thousands. I revisited it thirty years after, so I know. You think there are lots of wild horses down here in the coast valleys, but they are as nothing compared with those of the San Joaquin. Strange to say, the cows, when they went wild, went back into the lower mountains. Evidently they were better able to protect themselves there.

"In the country districts the ghouls and prowlers had been less in evidence, for I found many villages and towns untouched by fire. But they were filled by the pestilential dead, and I passed by without exploring them. It was near Lathrop that, out of my loneliness, I picked up a pair of collie dogs that were so newly free that they were urgently willing to return to their allegiance to man. These collies accompanied me for many years, and the strains of them are in those very dogs there that you boys have to-day. But in sixty years the collie strain has worked out. These brutes are more like domesticated wolves than anything else."

Hare-Lip rose to his feet, glanced to see that the goats were safe, and looked at the sun's position in the afternoon sky, advertising impatience at the prolixity of the old man's tale. Urged to hurry by Edwin, Granser went on.

"There is little more to tell. With my two dogs and my pony, and riding a horse I had managed to capture, I crossed the San Joaquin and went on to a wonderful valley in the Sierras called Yosemite. In the great hotel there I found a prodigious supply of tinned provisions. The pasture was abundant, as was the game, and the river that ran through the valley was full of trout. I remained there three years in an utter loneliness that none but a man who has once been highly civilized can understand. Then I could stand it no more. I felt that I was going crazy. Like the dog, I was a social animal and I needed my kind. I reasoned that since I had survived the plague, there was a possibility that others had survived. Also, I reasoned that after three years the plague germs must all be gone and the land be clean again.

"With my horse and dogs and pony, I set out. Again I crossed the San Joaquin Valley, the mountains beyond, and came down into Livermore Valley. The change in those three years was amazing. All the land had been splendidly tilled, and now I could scarcely recognize it, 'such was the sea of rank vegetation that had overrun the agricultural handiwork of man. You see, the wheat, the vegetables, and orchard trees had always been cared for and nursed by man, so that they were soft and tender. The weeds and wild bushes and such things, on the contrary, had always been fought by man, so that they were tough and resistant. As a result, when the hand of man was removed, the wild vegetation smothered and destroyed practically all the domesticated vegetation. The coyotes were greatly increased, and it was at this time that I first encountered wolves, straying in twos and threes and small packs down from the regions where they had always persisted.

"It was at Lake Temescal, not far from the one-time city of Oakland, that I came upon the first live human beings. Oh, my grandsons, how can I describe to you my emotion, when, astride my horse and dropping down the hillside to the lake, I saw the smoke of a campfire rising through the trees. Almost did my heart stop beating. I felt that I was going crazy. Then I heard the cry of a babe—a human babe. And dogs barked, and my dogs answered. I did not know but what I was the one human alive in the whole world. It could not be true that here were others—smoke, and the cry of a babe.

"Emerging on the lake, there, before my eyes, not a hundred yards away, I saw a man, a large man. He was standing on an outjutting rock and fishing. I was overcome. I stopped my horse. I tried to call out but could not. I waved my hand. It seemed to me that the man looked at me, but he did not appear to wave. Then I laid my head on my arms there in the saddle. I was afraid to look again, for I knew it was an hallucination, and I knew that if I looked the man would be gone. And so precious was the hallucination, that I wanted it to persist yet a little while. I knew, too, that as long as I did not look it would persist.

"Thus I remained, until I heard my dogs snarling, and a man's voice. What do you think the voice said? I will tell you. It said: 'Where in hell did you come from??'

"Those were the words, the exact words. That was what your other grandfather said to me, Hare-Lip, when he greeted me there on the shore of Lake Temescal fifty-seven years ago. And they were the most ineffable words I have ever heard. I opened my eyes, and there he stood before me, a large, dark, hairy man, heavy-jawed, slant-browed, fierce-eyed. How I got off my horse I do not know. But it seemed that the next I knew I was clasping his hand with both of mine and crying. I would have embraced him, but he was ever a narrow-minded, suspicious man, and he drew away from me. Yet did I cling to his hand and cry."

Granser's voice faltered and broke at the recollection, and the weak tears streamed down his cheeks while the boys looked on and giggled.

"Yet did I cry," he continued, "and desire to embrace him, though the Chauffeur was a brute, a perfect brute—the most abhorrent man I have ever known. His name was... strange, how I have forgotten his name. Everybody called him Chauffeur—it was the name of his occupation, and it stuck. That is how, to this day, the tribe he founded is called the Chauffeur Tribe.

"He was a violent, unjust man. Why the plague germs spared him I can never understand. It would seem, in spite of our old metaphysical notions about absolute justice, that there is no justice in the universe. Why did he live?—an iniquitous, moral monster, a blot on the face of nature, a cruel, relentless, bestial cheat as well. All he could talk about was motor cars, machinery, gasoline, and garages—and especially, and with huge delight, of his mean pilferings and sordid swindlings of the persons who had employed him in the days before the coming of the plague. And yet he was spared, while hundreds of millions, yea, billions, of better men were destroyed.

"I went on with him to his camp, and there I saw her, Vesta, the one woman. It was glorious and... pitiful. There she was, Vesta Van Warden, the young wife of John Van Warden, clad in rags, with marred and scarred and toil-calloused hands, bending over the campfire and doing scullion work—she, Vesta, who had been born to the purple of the greatest baronage of wealth the world had ever known. John Van Warden, her husband, worth one billion, eight hundred millions and President of the Board of Industrial Magnates, had been the ruler of America. Also, sitting on the International Board of Control, he had been one of the seven men who ruled the world. And she herself had come of equally noble stock. Her father, Philip Saxon, had been President of the Board of Industrial Magnates up to the time of his death. This office was in process of becoming hereditary, and had Philip Saxon had a son that son would have succeeded him. But his only child was Vesta, the perfect flower of generations of the highest culture this planet has ever produced. It was not until the engagement between Vesta and Van Warden took place, that Saxon indicated the latter as his successor. It was, I am sure, a political marriage. I have reason to believe that Vesta never really loved her husband in the mad passionate way of which the poets used to sing. It was more like the marriages that obtained among crowned heads in the days before they were displaced by the Magnates.

"And there she was, boiling fish-chowder in a soot-covered pot, her glorious eyes inflamed by the acrid smoke of the open fire. Hers was a sad story. She was the one survivor in a million, as I had been, as the Chauffeur had been. On a crowning eminence of the Alameda Hills, overlooking San Francisco Bay, Van Warden had built a vast summer palace. It was surrounded by a park of a thousand acres. When the plague broke out, Van Warden sent her there. Armed guards patrolled the boundaries of the park, and nothing entered in the way of provisions or even mail matter that was not first fumigated. And yet did the plague enter, killing the guards at their posts, the servants at their tasks, sweeping away the whole army of retainers—or, at least, all of them who did not flee to die elsewhere. So it was that Vesta found herself the sole living person in the palace that had become a charnel house.

"Now the Chauffeur had been one of the servants that ran away. Returning, two months afterward, he discovered Vesta in a little summer pavilion where there had been no deaths and where she had established herself. He was a brute. She was afraid, and she ran away and hid among the trees. That night, on foot, she fled into the mountains—she, whose tender feet and delicate body had never known the bruise of stones nor the scratch of briars. He followed, and that night he caught her. He struck her. Do you understand? He beat her with those terrible fists of his and made her his slave. It was she who had to gather the firewood, build the fires, cook, and do all the degrading camp-labor—she, who had never performed a menial act in her life. These things he compelled her to do, while he, a proper savage, elected to lie around camp and look on. He did nothing, absolutely nothing, except on occasion to hunt meat or catch fish."

"Good for Chauffeur," Hare-Lip commented in an undertone to the other boys. "I remember him before he died. He was a corker. But he did things, and he made things go. You know, Dad married his daughter, an' you ought to see the way he knocked the spots outa Dad. The Chauffeur was a son-of-a-gun. He made us kids stand around. Even when he was croaking he reached out for me, once, an' laid my head open with that long stick he kept always beside him."

Hare-Lip rubbed his bullet head reminiscently, and the boys returned to the old man, who was maundering ecstatically about Vesta, the squaw of the founder of the Chauffeur Tribe.

"And so I say to you that you cannot understand the awfulness of the situation. The Chauffeur was a servant, understand, a servant. And he cringed, with bowed head, to such as she. She was a lord of life, both by birth and by marriage. The destinies of millions, such as he, she carried in the hollow of her pink-white hand. And, in the days before the plague, the slightest contact with such as he would have been pollution. Oh, I have seen it. Once, I remember, there was Mrs. Goldwin, wife of one of the great magnates. It was on a landing stage, just as she was embarking in her private dirigible, that she dropped her parasol. A servant picked it up and made the mistake of handing it to her—to her, one of the greatest royal ladies of the land! She shrank back, as though he were a leper, and indicated her secretary to receive it. Also, she ordered her secretary to ascertain the creature's name and to see that he was immediately discharged from service. And such a woman was Vesta Van Warden. And her the Chauffeur beat and made his slave.

A "—Bill—that was it; Bill, the Chauffeur. That was his name. He was a wretched, primitive man, wholly devoid of the finer instincts and chivalrous promptings of a cultured soul. No, there is no absolute justice, for to him fell that wonder of womanhood, Vesta Van Warden. The grievous-ness of this you will never understand, my grandsons; for you are yourselves primitive little savages, unaware of aught else but savagery. Why should Vesta not have been mine? I was a man of culture and refinement, a professor in a great university. Even so, in the time before the plague, such was her exalted position, she would not have deigned to know that I existed. Mark, then, the abysmal degradation to which she fell at the hands of the Chauffeur. Nothing less than the destruction of all mankind had made it possible that I should know her, look in her eyes, converse with her, touch her hand—ay, and love her and know that her feelings toward me were very kindly. I have reason to believe that she, even she, would have loved me, there being no other man in the world except the Chauffeur. Why, when it destroyed eight billions of souls, did not the plague destroy just one more man, and that man the Chauffeur?

"Once, when the Chauffeur was away fishing, she begged me to kill him. With tears in her eyes she begged me to kill him. But he was a strong and violent man, and I was afraid. Afterwards, I talked with him. I offered him my horse, my pony, my dogs, all that I possessed, if he would give Vesta to me. And he grinned in my face and shook his head. He was very insulting. He said that in the old days he had been a servant, had been dirt under the feet of men like me and of women like Vesta, and that now he had the greatest lady in the land to be servant to him and cook his food and nurse his brats. 'You had your day before the plague,' he said; 'but this is my day, and a damned good day it is. I wouldn't trade back to the old times for anything.' Such words he spoke, but they are not his words. He was a vulgar, low-minded man, and vile oaths fell continually from his lips.

"Also, he told me that if he caught me making eyes at his woman he'd wring my neck and give her a beating as well. What was I to do? I was afraid. He was a brute. That first night, when I discovered the camp, Vesta and I had great talk about the things of our vanished world. We talked of art, and books, and poetry; and the Chauffeur listened and grinned and sneered. He was bored and angered by our way of speech which he did not comprehend, and finally he spoke up and said: 'And this is Vesta Van Warden, one-time wife of Van Warden the Magnate—a high and stuck-up beauty, who is now my squaw. Eh, Professor Smith, times is changed, times is changed. Here, you, woman, take off my moccasins, and lively about it. I want Professor Smith to see how well I have you trained.'

"I saw her clench her teeth, and the flame of revolt rise in her face. He drew back his gnarled fist to strike, and I was afraid, and sick at heart. I could do nothing to prevail against him. So I got up to go, and not be witness to such indignity. But the Chauffeur laughed and threatened me with a beating if I did not stay and behold. And I sat there, perforce, by the campfire on the shore of Lake Temescal, and saw Vesta, Vesta Van Warden, kneel and remove the moccasins of that grinning, hairy, apelike human brute.

"—Oh, you do not understand, my grandsons. You have never known anything else, and you do not understand.

"'Halter-broke and bridle-wise,' the Chauffeur gloated, while she performed that dreadful, menial task. 'A trifle balky at times, Professor, a trifle balky; but a clout alongside the jaw makes her as meek and gentle as a lamb.'

"And another time he said: 'We've got to start all over and replenish the earth and multiply. You're handicapped, Professor. You ain't got no wife, and we're up against a regular Garden-of-Eden proposition. But I ain't proud. I'll tell you what, Professor.' He pointed at their little infant, barely a year old. 'There's your wife, though you'll have to wait till she grows up. It's rich, ain't it? We're all equals here, and I'm the biggest toad in the splash. But I ain't stuck up—not I. I do you the honor, Professor Smith, the very great honor of betrothing to you my and Vesta Van Warden's daughter. Ain't it cussed bad that Van Warden ain't here to see?'"

VI

"I LIVED three weeks of infinite torment there in the Chauffeur's camp. And then, one day, tiring of me, or of what to him was my bad effect on Vesta, he told me that the year before, wandering through the Contra Costa Hills to the Straits of Carquinez, across the Straits he had seen a smoke. This meant that there were still other human beings, and that for three weeks he had kept this inestimably precious information from me. I departed at once, with my dogs and horses, and journeyed across the Contra Costa Hills to the Straits. I saw no smoke on the other side, but at Port Costa discovered a small steel barge on which I was able to embark my animals. Old canvas which I found served me for a sail, and a southerly breeze fanned me across the Straits and up to the ruins of Vallejo. Here, on the outskirts of the city, I found evidences of a recently occupied camp.

"Many clam-shells showed me why these humans had come to the shores of the Bay. This was the Santa Rosa Tribe, and I followed its track along the old railroad right of way across the salt marshes to Sonoma Valley. Here, at the old brickyard at Glen Ellen, I came upon the camp. There were eighteen souls all told. Two were old men, one of whom was Jones, a banker. The other was Harrison, a retired pawnbroker, who had taken for wife the matron of the State Hospital for the Insane at Napa. Of all the persons of the city of Napa, and of all the other towns and villages in that rich and populous valley, she had been the only-survivor. Next, there were the three young men—Cardiff and Hale, who had been farmers, and Wainwright, a common day-laborer. All three had found wives. To Hale, a crude, illiterate farmer, had fallen Isadore, the greatest prize, next to Vesta, of the women who came through the plague. She was one of the world's most noted singers, and the plague had caught her at San Francisco. She has talked with me for hours at a time, telling me of her adventures, until, at last, rescued by Hale in the Mendocino Forest Reserve, there had remained nothing for her to do but become his wife. But Hale was a good fellow, in spite of his illiteracy. He had a keen sense of justice and right-dealing, and she was far happier with him than was Vesta with the Chauffeur.

"The wives of Cardiff and Wainwright were ordinary women, accustomed to toil with strong constitutions—just the type for the wild new life which they were compelled to live. In addition were two adult idiots from the feeble-minded home at El-dredge, and five or six young children and infants born after the formation of the Santa Rosa Tribe. Also, there was Bertha. She was a good woman, Hare-Lip, in spite of the sneers of your father. Her I took for wife. She was the mother of your father, Edwin, and of yours, Hoo-Hoo. And it was our daughter, Vera, who married your father, Hare-Lip—your father, Sandow, who was the oldest son of Vesta Van Warden and the Chauffeur.

"And so it was that I became the nineteenth member of the Santa Rosa Tribe. There were only two outsiders added after me. One was Mungerson, descended from the Magnates, who wandered alone in the wilds of Northern California for eight years before he came south and joined us. He it was who waited twelve years more before he married my daughter, Mary. The other was Johnson, the man who founded the Utah Tribe. That was where he came from, Utah, a country that lies very far away from here, across the great deserts, to the east. It was not until twenty-seven years after the plague that Johnson reached California. In all that Utah region he reported but three survivors, himself one, and all men. For many years these three men lived and hunted together, until, at last, desperate, fearing that with them the human race would perish utterly from the planet, they headed westward on the possibility of finding women survivors in California. Johnson alone came through the great desert, where his two companions died. He was forty-six years old when he joined us, and he married the fourth daughter of Isadore and Hale, and his eldest son married your aunt, Hare-Lip, who was the third daughter of Vesta and the Chauffeur. Johnson was a strong man, with a will of his own. And it was because of this that he seceded from the Santa Rosans and formed the Utah Tribe at San José. It is a small tribe—there are only nine in it; but, though he is dead, such was his influence and the strength of his breed, that it will grow into a strong tribe and play a leading part in the recivilization of the planet.

"There are only two other tribes that we know of—the Los Angelitos and the Carmelitos. The latter started from one man and woman. He was called Lopez, and he was descended from the ancient Mexicans and was very black. He was a cowherd in the ranges beyond Carmel, and his wife was a maidservant in the great Del Monte Hotel. It was seven years before we first got in touch with the Los Ange-litos. They have a good country down there, but it is too warm. I estimate the present population of the world at between three hundred and fifty and four hundred—provided, of course, that there are no scattered little tribes elsewhere in the world. If there be such, we have not heard from them. Since Johnson crossed the desert from Utah, no word nor sign has come from the East or anywhere else. The great world which I knew in my boyhood and early manhood is gone. It has ceased to be. I am the last man who was alive in the days of the plague and who knows the wonders of that far-off time. We, who mastered the planet—its earth, and sea, and sky—and who were as very gods, now live in primitive savagery along the water courses of this California country.

"But we are increasing rapidly—your sister, Hare-Lip, already has four children. We are increasing rapidly and making ready for a new climb toward civilization. In time, pressure of population will compel us to spread out, and a hundred generations from now we may expect our descendants to start across the Sierras, oozing slowly along, generation by generation, over the great continent to the colonization of the East—a new Aryan drift around the world.

"But it will be slow, very slow; we have so far to climb. We fell so hopelessly far. If only one physicist or one chemist had survived! But it was not to be, and we have forgotten everything. The Chauffeur started working in iron. He made the forge which we use to this day. But he was a lazy man, and when he died he took with him all he knew of metals and machinery. What was I to know of such things? I was a classical scholar, not a chemist.. The other men who survived were not educated. Only two things did the Chauffeur accomplish—the brewing of strong drink and the growing of tobacco. It was while he was drunk, once, that he killed Vesta. I firmly believe that he killed Vesta in a fit of drunken cruelty though he always maintained that she fell into the lake and was drowned.

"And, my grandsons, let me warn you against the medicine-men. They call themselves doctors, travestying what was once a noble profession, but in reality they are medicine-men, devil-devil men, and they make for superstition and darkness. They are cheats and liars. But so debased and degraded are we, that we believe their lies. They, too, will increase in numbers as we increase, and they will strive to rule us. Yet are they liars and charlatans. Look at young Cross-Eyes, posing as a doctor, selling charms against sickness, giving good hunting, exchanging promises of fair weather for good meat and skins, sending the death-stick, performing a thousand abominations. Yet I say to you, that when he says he can do these things, he lies. I, Professor Smith, Professor James Howard Smith, say that he lies. I have told him so to his teeth. Why has he not sent me the death-stick? Because he knows that with me it is without avail. But you, Hare-Lip, so deeply are you sunk in black superstition that did you awake this night and find the death-stick beside you, you would surely die. And you would die, not because of any virtues in the stick, but because you are a savage with the dark and clouded mind of a savage.

"The doctors must be destroyed, and all that was lost must be discovered over again. Wherefore, earnestly, I repeat unto you certain things which you must remember and tell to your children after you. You must tell them that when water is made hot by fire, there resides in it a wonderful thing called steam, which is stronger than ten thousand men and which can do all man's work for him. There are other very useful things. In the lightning flash resides a similarly strong servant of man, which was of old his slave and which some day will be his slave again.

"Quite a different thing is the alphabet. It is what enables me to know the meaning of fine markings, whereas you boys know only rude picture-writing. In that dry cave on Telegraph Hill, where you see me often go when the tribe is down by the sea, I have stored many books. In them is great wisdom. Also, with them, I have placed a key to the alphabet, so that one who knows picture-writing may also know print. Some day men will read again; and then, if no accident has befallen my cave, they will know that Professor James Howard Smith once lived and saved for them the knowledge of the ancients.

"There is another little device that men inevitably will rediscover. It is called gunpowder. It was what enabled us to kill surely and at long distances. Certain things which are found in the ground, when combined in the right proportions, will make this gunpowder. What these things are, I have forgotten, or else I never knew. But I wish I did know. Then would I make powder, and then would I certainly kill Cross-Eyes and rid the land of superstition—"

"After I am man-grown I am going to give Cross-Eyes all the goats, and meat, and skins I can get, so that he'll teach me to be a doctor," Hoo-Hoo asserted. "And when I know, I'll make everybody else sit up and take notice. They'll get down in the dirt to me, you bet."

The old man nodded his head solemnly, and murmured:

"Strange it is to hear the vestiges and remnants of the complicated Aryan speech falling from the lips of a filthy little skin-clad savage. All the world is topsy-turvy. And it has been topsy-turvy ever since the plague."

"You won't make me sit up," Hare-Lip boasted to the would-be medicine-man. "If I paid you for a sending of the death-stick and it didn't work, I'd bust in your head—understand, you Hoo-Hoo, you?"

"I'm going to get Granser to remember this here gunpowder stuff," Edwin said softly, "and then I'll have you all on the run. You, Hare-Lip, will do my fighting for me and get my meat for me, and you, Hoo-Hoo, will send the death-stick for me and make everybody afraid. And if I catch Hare-Lip trying to bust your head, Hoo-Hoo, I'll fix him with that same gunpowder. Granser ain't such a fool as you think, and I'm going to listen to him and some day I'll be boss over the whole bunch of you."

The old man shook his head sadly, and said:

"The gunpowder will come. Nothing can stop it—the same old story over and over. Man will increase, and men will fight. The gunpowder will enable men to kill millions of men, and in this way only, by fire and blood, will a new civilization, in some remote day, be evolved. And of what profit will it be? Just as the old civilization passed, so will the new. It may take fifty thousand years to build, but it will pass. All things pass. Only remain cosmic force and matter, ever in flux, ever acting and reacting and realizing the eternal types—the priest, the soldier, and the king. Out of the mouths of babes comes the wisdom of all the ages. Some will fight, some will rule, some will pray; and all the rest will toil and suffer sore while on their bleeding carcasses is reared again, and yet again, without end, the amazing beauty and surpassing wonder of the civilized state. It were just as well that I destroyed those cave-stored books—whether they remain or perish, all their old truths will be discovered, their old lies lived and handed down. What is the profit—"

Hare-Lip leaped to his feet, giving a quick glance at the pasturing goats and the afternoon sun.

"Gee!" he muttered to Edwin, "The old geezer gets more long-winded every day. Let's pull for camp."

While the other two, aided by the dogs, assembled the goats and started them for the trail through the forest, Edwin stayed by the old man and guided him in the same direction. When they reached the old right of way, Edwin stopped suddenly and looked back. Hare-Lip and Hoo-Hoo and the dogs and the goats passed on. Edwin was looking at a small herd of wild horses which had come down on the hard sand. There were at least twenty of them, young colts and yearlings and mares, led by a beautiful stallion which stood in the foam at the edge of the surf, with arched neck and bright wild eyes, sniffing the salt air from off the sea.

"What is it?" Granser queried.

"Horses," was the answer. "First time I ever seen 'em on the beach. It's the mountain lions getting thicker and thicker and driving 'em down."

The low sun shot red shafts of light, fan-shaped, up from a cloud-tumbled horizon. And close at hand, in the white waste of shore-lashed waters, the sea-lions, bellowing their old primeval chant, hauled up out of the sea on the black rocks and fought and loved.

"Come on, Granser," Edwin prompted. And old man and boy, skin-clad and barbaric, turned and went along the right of way into the forest in the wake of the goats.

THE END

THE GAME

CHAPTER I

Many patterns of carpet lay rolled out before them on the floor—two of Brussels showed the beginning of their quest, and its ending in that direction; while a score of ingrains lured their eyes and prolonged the debate between desire pocket-book. The head of the department did them the honor of waiting upon them himself—or did Joe the honor, as she well knew, for she had noted the open-mouthed awe of the elevator boy who brought them up. Nor had she been blind to the marked respect shown Joe by the urchins and groups of young fellows on corners, when she walked with him in their own neighborhood down at the west end of the town.

But the head of the department was called away to the telephone, and in her mind the splendid promise of the carpets and the irk of the pocket-book were thrust aside by a greater doubt and anxiety.

"But I don't see what you find to like in it, Joe," she said softly, the note of insistence in her words betraying recent and unsatisfactory discussion.

For a fleeting moment a shadow darkened his boyish face, to be replaced by the glow of tenderness. He was only a boy, as she was only a girl—two young things on the threshold of life, house-renting and buying carpets together.

"What's the good of worrying?" he questioned. "It's the last go, the very last."

He smiled at her, but she saw on his lips the unconscious and all but breathed sigh of renunciation, and with the instinctive monopoly of woman for her mate, she feared this thing she did not understand and which gripped his life so strongly.

"You know the go with O'Neil cleared the last payment on mother's house," he went on. "And that's off my mind. Now this last with Ponta will give me a hundred dollars in bank—an even hundred, that's the purse—for you and me to start on, a nest-egg."

She disregarded the money appeal. "But you like it, this—this 'game' you call it. Why?"

He lacked speech-expression. He expressed himself with his hands, at his work, and with his body and the play of his muscles in the squared ring; but to tell with his own lips the charm of the squared ring was beyond him. Yet he essayed, and haltingly at first, to express what he felt and analyzed when playing the Game at the supreme summit of existence.

"All I know, Genevieve, is that you feel good in the ring when you've got the man where you want him, when he's had a punch up both sleeves waiting for you and you've never given him an opening to land 'em, when you've landed your own little punch an' he's goin' groggy, an' holdin' on, an' the referee's dragging him off so's you can go in an' finish 'm, an' all the house is shouting an' tearin' itself loose, an' you know you're the best man, an' that you played m' fair an' won out because you're the best man. I tell you—"

He ceased brokenly, alarmed by his own volubility and by Genevieve's look of alarm. As he talked she had watched his face while fear dawned in her own. As he described the moment of moments to her, on his inward vision were lined the tottering man, the lights, the shouting house, and he swept out and away from her on this tide of life that was beyond her comprehension, menacing, irresistible, making her love pitiful and weak. The Joe she knew receded, faded, became lost. The fresh boyish face was gone, the tenderness of the eyes, the sweetness of the mouth with its curves and pictured corners. It was a man's face she saw, a face of steel, tense and immobile; a mouth of steel, the lips like the jaws of a trap; eyes of steel, dilated, intent, and the light in them and the glitter were the light and glitter of steel. The face of a man, and she had known only his boy face. This face she did not know at all.

And yet, while it frightened her, she was vaguely stirred with pride in him. His masculinity, the masculinity of the fighting male, made its inevitable appeal to her, a female, moulded by all her heredity to seek out the strong man for mate, and to lean against the wall of his strength. She did not understand this force of his being that rose mightier than her love and laid its compulsion upon him; and yet, in her woman's heart she was aware of the sweet pang which told her that for her sake, for Love's own sake, he had surrendered to her, abandoned all that portion of his life, and with this one last fight would never fight again.

"Mrs. Silverstein doesn't like prize-fighting," she said. "She's down on it, and she knows something, too."

He smiled indulgently, concealing a hurt, not altogether new, at her persistent inappreciation of this side of his nature and life in which he took the greatest pride. It was to him power and achievement, earned by his own effort and hard work; and in the moment when he had offered himself and all that he was to Genevieve, it was this, and this alone, that he was proudly conscious of laying at her feet.

It was the merit of work performed, a guerdon of manhood finer and greater than any other man could offer, and it had been to him his justification and right to possess her. And she had not understood it then, as she did not understand it now, and he might well have wondered what else she found in him to make him worthy.

"Mrs. Silverstein is a dub, and a softy, and a knocker," he said good-humoredly. "What's she know about such things, anyway? I tell you it is good, and healthy, too,"—this last as an afterthought. "Look at me. I tell you I have to live clean to be in condition like this. I live cleaner than she does, or her old man, or anybody you know—baths, rub-downs, exercise, regular hours, good food and no makin' a pig of myself, no drinking, no smoking, nothing that'll hurt me. Why, I live cleaner than you, Genevieve—"

"Honest, I do," he hastened to add at sight of her shocked face. "I don't mean water an' soap, but look there." His hand closed reverently but firmly on her arm. "Soft, you're all soft, all over. Not like mine. Here, feel this."

He pressed the ends of her fingers into his hard arm-muscles until she winced from the hurt.

"Hard all over just like that," he went on. "Now that's what I call clean. Every bit of flesh an' blood an' muscle is clean right down to the bones—and they're clean, too. No soap and water only on the skin, but clean all the way in. I tell you it feels clean. It knows it's clean itself. When I wake up in the morning an' go to work, every drop of blood and bit of meat is shouting right out that it is clean. Oh, I tell you—"

He paused with swift awkwardness, again confounded by his

unwonted flow of speech. Never in his life had he been stirred to such utterance, and never in his life had there been cause to be so stirred. For it was the Game that had been questioned, its verity and worth, the Game itself, the biggest thing in the world—or what had been the biggest thing in the world until that chance afternoon and that chance purchase in Silverstein's candy store, when Genevieve loomed suddenly colossal in his life, overshadowing all other things. He was beginning to see, though vaguely, the sharp conflict between woman and career, between a man's work in the world and woman's need of the man. But he was not capable of generalization. He saw only the antagonism between the concrete, flesh-and-blood Genevieve and the great, abstract, living Game. Each resented the other, each claimed him; he was torn with the strife, and yet drifted helpless on the currents of their contention.

His words had drawn Genevieve's gaze to his face, and she had pleasured in the clear skin, the clear eyes, the cheek soft and smooth as a girl's. She saw the force of his argument and disliked it accordingly. She revolted instinctively against this Game which drew him away from her, robbed her of part of him. It was a rival she did not understand. Nor could she understand its seductions. Had it been a woman rival, another girl, knowledge and light and sight would have been hers. As it was, she grappled in the dark with an intangible adversary about which she knew nothing. What truth she felt in his speech made the Game but the more formidable.

A sudden conception of her weakness came to her. She felt pity for herself, and sorrow. She wanted him, all of him, her woman's need would not be satisfied with less; and he eluded her, slipped away here and there from the embrace with which she tried to clasp him. Tears swam into her eyes, and her lips trembled, turning defeat into victory, routing the all-potent Game with the strength of her weakness.

"Don't, Genevieve, don't," the boy pleaded, all contrition, though he was confused and dazed. To his masculine mind there was nothing relevant about her break-down; yet all else was forgotten at sight of her tears.

She smiled forgiveness through her wet eyes, and though he knew of nothing for which to be forgiven, he melted utterly. His hand went out impulsively to hers, but she avoided the clasp by a sort of bodily stiffening and chill, the while the eyes smiled still more gloriously.

"Here comes Mr. Clausen," she said, at the same time, by some transforming alchemy of woman, presenting to the newcomer eyes that showed no hint of moistness.

"Think I was never coming back, Joe?" queried the head of the department, a pink-and-white-faced man, whose austere side-whiskers were belied by genial little eyes.

"Now let me see—hum, yes, we was discussing ingrains," he continued briskly. "That tasty little pattern there catches your eye, don't it now, eh? Yes, yes, I know all about it. I set up housekeeping when I was getting fourteen a week. But nothing's too good for the little nest, eh? Of course I know, and it's only seven cents more, and the dearest is the cheapest, I say. Tell you what I'll do, Joe,"—this with a burst of philanthropic impulsiveness and a confidential lowering of voice,—"seein's it's you, and I wouldn't do it for anybody else, I'll reduce it to five cents. Only,"—here his voice became impressively solemn,—"only you mustn't ever tell how much you really did pay."

"Sewed, lined, and laid—of course that's included," he said, after Joe and Genevieve had conferred together and announced their decision.

"And the little nest, eh?" he queried. "When do you spread your wings and fly away? To-morrow! So soon? Beautiful! Beautiful!"

He rolled his eyes ecstatically for a moment, then beamed upon them with a fatherly air.

Joe had replied sturdily enough, and Genevieve had blushed prettily; but both felt that it was not exactly proper. Not alone because of the privacy and holiness of the subject, but because of what might have been prudery in the middle class, but which in them was the modesty and reticence found in individuals of the working class when they strive after clean living and morality.

Mr. Clausen accompanied them to the elevator, all smiles, patronage, and beneficence, while the clerks turned their heads to follow Joe's retreating figure.

"And to-night, Joe?" Mr. Clausen asked anxiously, as they waited at the shaft. "How do you feel? Think you'll do him?"

"Sure," Joe answered. "Never felt better in my life."

"You feel all right, eh? Good! Good! You see, I was just a-wonderin'—you know, ha! ha!—goin' to get married and the rest—thought you might be unstrung, eh, a trifle?—nerves just a bit off, you know. Know how gettin' married is myself. But you're all right, eh? Of course you are. No use asking you that. Ha! ha! Well, good luck, my boy! I know you'll win. Never had the least doubt, of course, of course."

"And good-by, Miss Pritchard," he said to Genevieve, gallantly handing her into the elevator. "Hope you call often. Will be charmed—charmed—I assure you."

"Everybody calls you 'Joe'," she said reproachfully, as the car dropped downward. "Why don't they call you 'Mr. Fleming'? That's no more than proper."

But he was staring moodily at the elevator boy and did not seem to hear.

"What's the matter, Joe?" she asked, with a tenderness the power of which to thrill him she knew full well.

"Oh, nothing," he said. "I was only thinking—and wishing."

"Wishing?—what?" Her voice was seduction itself, and her eyes would have melted stronger than he, though they failed in calling his up to them.

Then, deliberately, his eyes lifted to hers. "I was wishing you could see me fight just once."

She made a gesture of disgust, and his face fell. It came to her sharply that the rival had thrust between and was bearing him away.

"I—I'd like to," she said hastily with an effort, striving after that sympathy which weakens the strongest men and draws their heads to women's breasts.

"Will you?"

Again his eyes lifted and looked into hers. He meant it—she knew that. It seemed a challenge to the greatness of her love.

"It would be the proudest moment of my life," he said simply.

It may have been the apprehensiveness of love, the wish to meet his need for her sympathy, and the desire to see the Game face to face for wisdom's sake,—and it may have been the clarion call of adventure ringing through the narrow confines of uneventful existence; for a great daring thrilled through her, and she said, just as simply, "I will."

"I didn't think you would, or I wouldn't have asked," he confessed, as they walked out to the sidewalk.

"But can't it be done?" she asked anxiously, before her resolution could cool.

"Oh, I can fix that; but I didn't think you would."

"I didn't think you would," he repeated, still amazed, as he helped her upon the electric car and felt in his pocket for the fare.

CHAPTER II

Genevieve and Joe were working-class aristocrats. In an environment made up largely of sordidness and wretchedness they had kept themselves unsullied and wholesome. Theirs was a self-respect, a regard for the niceties and clean things of life, which had held them aloof from their kind. Friends did not come to them easily; nor had either ever possessed a really intimate friend, a heart-companion with whom to chum and have things in common. The social instinct was strong in them, yet they had remained lonely because they could not satisfy that instinct and at that same time satisfy their desire for cleanness and decency.

If ever a girl of the working class had led the sheltered life, it was Genevieve. In the midst of roughness and brutality, she had shunned all that was rough and brutal. She saw but what she chose to see, and she chose always to see the best, avoiding coarseness and uncouthness without effort, as a matter of instinct. To begin with, she had been peculiarly unexposed. An only child, with an invalid mother upon whom she attended, she had not joined in the street games and frolics of the children of the neighbourhood. Her father, a mild-tempered, narrow-chested, anæmic little clerk, domestic because of his inherent disability to mix with men, had done his full share toward giving the home an atmosphere of sweetness and tenderness.

An orphan at twelve, Genevieve had gone straight from her father's funeral to live with the Silversteins in their rooms above the candy store; and here, sheltered by kindly aliens, she earned her keep and clothes by waiting on the shop. Being Gentile, she was especially necessary to the Silversteins, who would not run the business themselves when the day of their Sabbath came round.

And here, in the uneventful little shop, six maturing years had slipped by. Her acquaintances were few. She had elected to have no girl chum for the reason that no satisfactory girl had appeared. Nor did she choose to walk with the young fellows of the neighbourhood, as was the custom of girls from their fifteenth year. "That stuck-up doll-face," was the way the girls of the neighbourhood described her; and though she earned their enmity by her beauty and aloofness, she none the less commanded their respect. "Peaches and cream," she was called by the young men—though softly and amongst themselves, for they were afraid of arousing the ire of the other girls, while they stood in awe of Genevieve, in a dimly religious way, as a something mysteriously beautiful and unapproachable.

For she was indeed beautiful. Springing from a long line of American descent, she was one of those wonderful working-class blooms which occasionally appear, defying all precedent of forebears and environment, apparently without cause or explanation. She was a beauty in color, the blood spraying her white skin so deliciously as to earn for her the apt description, "peaches and cream." She was a beauty in the regularity of her features; and, if for no other reason, she was a beauty in the mere delicacy of the lines on which she was moulded. Quiet, low-voiced, stately, and dignified, she somehow had the knack of dress, and but befitted her beauty and dignity with anything she put on. Withal, she was sheerly feminine, tender and soft and clinging, with the smouldering passion of the mate and the motherliness of the woman. But this side of her nature had lain dormant through the years, waiting for the mate to appear.

Then Joe came into Silverstein's shop one hot Saturday afternoon to cool himself with ice-cream soda. She had not noticed his entrance, being busy with one other customer, an urchin of six or seven who gravely analyzed his desires before the show-case wherein truly generous and marvellous candy creations reposed under a cardboard announcement, "Five for Five Cents."

She had heard, "Ice-cream soda, please," and had herself asked, "What flavor?" without seeing his face. For that matter, it was not a custom of hers to notice young men. There was something about them she did not understand. The way they looked at her made her uncomfortable, she knew not why; while there was an uncouthness and roughness about them that did not please her. As yet, her imagination had been untouched by man. The young fellows she had seen had held no lure for her, had been without meaning to her. In short, had she been asked to give one reason for the existence of men on the earth, she would have been nonplussed for a reply.

As she emptied the measure of ice-cream into the glass, her casual glance rested on Joe's face, and she experienced on the instant a pleasant feeling of satisfaction. The next instant his eyes were upon her face, her eyes had dropped, and she was turning away toward the soda fountain. But at the fountain, filling the glass, she was impelled to look at him again—but for no more than an instant, for this time she found his eyes already upon her, waiting to meet hers, while on his face was a frankness of interest that caused her quickly to look away.

That such pleasingness would reside for her in any man astonished her. "What a pretty boy," she thought to herself, innocently and instinctively trying to ward off the power to hold and draw her that lay behind the mere prettiness. "Besides, he isn't pretty," she thought, as she placed the glass before him, received the silver dime in payment, and for the third time looked into his eyes. Her vocabulary was limited, and she knew little of the worth of words; but the strong masculinity of his boy's face told her that the term was inappropriate.

"He must be handsome, then," was her next thought, as she again dropped her eyes before his. But all good-looking men were called handsome, and that term, too, displeased her. But whatever it was, he was good to see, and she was irritably aware of a desire to look at him again and again.

As for Joe, he had never seen anything like this girl across the counter. While he was wiser in natural philosophy than she, and could have given immediately the reason for woman's existence on the earth, nevertheless woman had no part in his cosmos. His imagination was as untouched by woman as the girl's was by man. But his imagination was touched now, and the woman was Genevieve. He had never dreamed a girl could be so beautiful, and he could not keep his eyes from her face. Yet every time he looked at her, and her eyes met his, he felt painful embarrassment, and would have looked away had not her eyes dropped so quickly.

But when, at last, she slowly lifted her eyes and held their gaze steadily, it was his own eyes that dropped, his own cheek that mantled red. She was much less embarrassed than he, while she betrayed her embarrassment not at all. She was aware of a flutter within, such as she had never known before, but in no way did it disturb her outward serenity. Joe, on the contrary, was obviously awkward and delightfully miserable.

Neither knew love, and all that either was aware was an

overwhelming desire to look at the other. Both had been troubled and roused, and they were drawing together with the sharpness and imperativeness of uniting elements. He toyed with his spoon, and flushed his embarrassment over his soda, but lingered on; and she spoke softly, dropped her eyes, and wove her witchery about him.

But he could not linger forever over a glass of ice-cream soda, while he did not dare ask for a second glass. So he left her to remain in the shop in a waking trance, and went away himself down the street like a somnambulist. Genevieve dreamed through the afternoon and knew that she was in love. Not so with Joe. He knew only that he wanted to look at her again, to see her face. His thoughts did not get beyond this, and besides, it was scarcely a thought, being more a dim and inarticulate desire.

The urge of this desire he could not escape. Day after day it worried him, and the candy shop and the girl behind the counter continually obtruded themselves. He fought off the desire. He was afraid and ashamed to go back to the candy shop. He solaced his fear with, "I ain't a ladies' man." Not once, nor twice, but scores of times, he muttered the thought to himself, but it did no good. And by the middle of the week, in the evening, after work, he came into the shop. He tried to come in carelessly and casually, but his whole carriage advertised the strong effort of will that compelled his legs to carry his reluctant body thither. Also, he was shy, and awkwarder than ever. Genevieve, on the contrary, was serener than ever, though fluttering most alarmingly within. He was incapable of speech, mumbled his order, looked anxiously at the clock, despatched his ice-cream soda in tremendous haste, and was gone.

She was ready to weep with vexation. Such meagre reward for four days' waiting, and assuming all the time that she loved! He was a nice boy and all that, she knew, but he needn't have been in so disgraceful a hurry. But Joe had not reached the corner before he wanted to be back with her again. He just wanted to look at her. He had no thought that it was love. Love? That was when young fellows and girls walked out together. As for him—And then his desire took sharper shape, and he discovered that that was the very thing he wanted her to do. He wanted to see her, to look at her, and well could he do all this if she but walked out with him. Then that was why the young fellows and girls walked out together, he mused, as the week-end drew near. He had remotely considered this walking out to be a mere form or observance preliminary to matrimony. Now he saw the deeper wisdom in it, wanted it himself, and concluded therefrom that he was in love.

Both were now of the same mind, and there could be but the one ending; and it was the mild nine days' wonder of Genevieve's neighborhood when she and Joe walked out together.

Both were blessed with an avarice of speech, and because of it their courtship was a long one. As he expressed himself in action, she expressed herself in repose and control, and by the love-light in her eyes—though this latter she would have suppressed in all maiden modesty had she been conscious of the speech her heart printed so plainly there. "Dear" and "darling" were too terribly intimate for them to achieve quickly; and, unlike most mating couples, they did not overwork the love-words. For a long time they were content to walk together in the evenings, or to sit side by side on a bench in the park, neither uttering a word for an hour at a time, merely gazing into each other's eyes, too faintly luminous in the starshine to be a cause for self-consciousness and embarrassment.

He was as chivalrous and delicate in his attention as any knight to his lady. When they walked along the street, he was careful to be on the outside,—somewhere he had heard that this was the proper thing to do,—and when a crossing to the opposite side of the street put him on the inside, he swiftly side-stepped behind her to gain the outside again. He carried her parcels for her, and once, when rain threatened, her umbrella. He had never heard of the custom of sending flowers to one's lady-love, so he sent Genevieve fruit instead. There was utility in fruit. It was good to eat. Flowers never entered his mind, until, one day, he noticed a pale rose in her hair. It drew his gaze again and again. It was her hair, therefore the presence of the flower interested him. Again, it interested him because she had chosen to put it there. For these reasons he was led to observe the rose more closely. He discovered that the effect in itself was beautiful, and it fascinated him. His ingenuous delight in it was a delight to her, and a new and mutual love-thrill was theirs—because of a flower. Straightway he became a lover of flowers. Also, he became an inventor in gallantry. He sent her a bunch of violets. The idea was his own. He had never heard of a man sending flowers to a woman. Flowers were used for decorative purposes, also for funerals. He sent Genevieve flowers nearly every day, and so far as he was concerned the idea was original, as positive an invention as ever arose in the mind of man.

He was tremulous in his devotion to her—as tremulous as was she in her reception of him. She was all that was pure and good, a holy of holies not lightly to be profaned even by what might possibly be the too ardent reverence of a devotee. She was a being wholly different from any he had ever known. She was not as other girls. It never entered his head that she was of the same clay as his own sisters, or anybody's sister. She was more than mere girl, than mere woman. She was—well, she was Genevieve, a being of a class by herself, nothing less than a miracle of creation.

And for her, in turn, there was in him but little less of illusion. Her judgment of him in minor things might be critical (while his judgment of her was sheer worship, and had in it nothing critical at all); but in her judgment of him as a whole she forgot the sum of the parts, and knew him only as a creature of wonder, who gave meaning to life, and for whom she could die as willingly as she could live. She often beguiled her waking dreams of him with fancied situations, wherein, dying for him, she at last adequately expressed the love she felt for him, and which, living, she knew she could never fully express.

Their love was all fire and dew. The physical scarcely entered into it, for such seemed profanation. The ultimate physical facts of their relation were something which they never considered. Yet the immediate physical facts they knew, the immediate yearnings and raptures of the flesh—the touch of finger tips on hand or arm, the momentary pressure of a hand-clasp, the rare lip-caress of a kiss, the tingling thrill of her hair upon his cheek, of her hand lightly thrusting back the locks from above his eyes. All this they knew, but also, and they knew not why, there seemed a hint of sin about these caresses and sweet bodily contacts.

There were times when she felt impelled to throw her arms around him in a very abandonment of love, but always some sanctity restrained her. At such moments she was distinctly and unpleasantly aware of some unguessed sin that lurked within her. It was wrong, undoubtedly wrong, that she should wish to caress her lover in so unbecoming a fashion. No self-respecting girl could dream of doing such a thing. It was unwomanly. Besides, if she had done it, what would he have thought of it? And while she contemplated so horrible a catastrophe, she seemed to shrivel and wilt in a furnace of secret shame.

Nor did Joe escape the prick of curious desires, chiefest among which, perhaps, was the desire to hurt Genevieve. When, after long and tortuous degrees, he had achieved the bliss of putting his arm round her waist, he felt spasmodic impulses to make the embrace crushing, till she should cry out with the hurt. It was not his nature to wish to hurt any living thing. Even in the ring, to hurt was never the intention of any blow he struck. In such case he played the Game, and the goal of the Game was to down an antagonist and keep that antagonist down for a space of ten seconds. So he never struck merely to hurt; the hurt was incidental to the end, and the end was quite another matter. And yet here, with this girl he loved, came the desire to hurt. Why, when with thumb and forefinger he had ringed her wrist, he should desire to contract that ring till it crushed, was beyond him. He could not understand, and felt that he was discovering depths of brutality in his nature of which he had never dreamed.

Once, on parting, he threw his arms around her and swiftly drew her against him. Her gasping cry of surprise and pain brought him to his senses and left him there very much embarrassed and still trembling with a vague and nameless delight. And she, too, was trembling. In the hurt itself, which was the essence of the vigorous embrace, she had found delight; and again she knew sin, though she knew not its nature nor why it should be sin.

Came the day, very early in their walking out, when Silverstein chanced upon Joe in his store and stared at him with saucer-eyes. Came likewise the scene, after Joe had departed, when the maternal feelings of Mrs. Silverstein found vent in a diatribe against all prize-fighters and against Joe Fleming in particular. Vainly had Silverstein striven to stay the spouse's wrath. There was need for her wrath. All the maternal feelings were hers but none of the maternal rights.

Genevieve was aware only of the diatribe; she knew a flood of abuse was pouring from the lips of the Jewess, but she was too stunned to hear the details of the abuse. Joe, her Joe, was Joe Fleming the prize-fighter. It was abhorrent, impossible, too grotesque to be believable. Her clear-eyed, girl-cheeked Joe might be anything but a prize-fighter. She had never seen one, but he in no way resembled her conception of what a prize-fighter must be—the human brute with tiger eyes and a streak for a forehead. Of course she had heard of Joe Fleming—who in West Oakland had not?—but that there should be anything more than a coincidence of names had never crossed her mind.

She came out of her daze to hear Mrs. Silverstein's hysterical sneer, "keepin' company vit a bruiser." Next, Silverstein and his wife fell to differing on "noted" and "notorious" as applicable to her lover.

"But he iss a good boy," Silverstein was contending. "He make der money, an' he safe der money."

"You tell me dat!" Mrs. Silverstein screamed. "Vat you know? You know too much. You spend good money on der prize-fighters. How you know? Tell me dat! How you know?"

"I know vat I know," Silverstein held on sturdily—a thing Genevieve had never before seen him do when his wife was in her tantrums. "His fader die, he go to work in Hansen's sail-loft. He haf six brudders an' sisters younger as he iss. He iss der liddle fader. He vork hard, all der time. He buy der pread an' der meat, an' pay der rent. On Saturday night he bring home ten dollar. Den Hansen gif him twelve dollar—vat he do? He iss der liddle fader, he bring it home to der mudder. He vork all der time, he get twenty dollar—vat he do? He bring it home. Der liddle brudders an' sisters go to school, vear good clothes, haf better pread an' meat;

der mudder lif fat, dere iss joy in der eye, an' she iss proud of her good boy Joe.

"But he haf der beautiful body—ach, Gott, der beautiful body!—stronger as der ox, k-vicker as der tiger-cat, der head cooler as der ice-box, der eyes vat see eferytings, k-vick, just like dat. He put on der gloves vit der boys at Hansen's loft, he put on der gloves vit de boys at der varehouse. He go before der club; he knock out der Spider, k-vick, one punch, just like dat, der first time. Der purse iss five dollar—vat he do? He bring it home to der mudder.

"He go many times before der clubs; he get many purses—ten dollar, fifty dollar, one hundred dollar. Vat he do? Tell me dat! Quit der job at Hansen's? Haf der good time vit der boys? No, no; he iss der good boy. He vork efery day. He fight at night before der clubs. He say, 'Vat for I pay der rent, Silverstein?'—to me, Silverstein, he say dat. Nefer mind vat I say, but he buy der good house for der mudder. All der time he vork at Hansen's and fight before der clubs to pay for der house. He buy der piano for der sisters, der carpets, der pictures on der vall. An' he iss all der time straight. He bet on himself—dat iss der good sign. Ven der man bets on himself dat is der time you bet too—"

Here Mrs. Silverstein groaned her horror of gambling, and her husband, aware that his eloquence had betrayed him, collapsed into voluble assurances that he was ahead of the game. "An' all because of Joe Fleming," he concluded. "I back him efery time to vin."

But Genevieve and Joe were preëminently mated, and nothing, not even this terrible discovery, could keep them apart. In vain Genevieve tried to steel herself against him; but she fought herself, not him. To her surprise she discovered a thousand excuses for him, found him lovable as ever; and she entered into his life to be his destiny, and to control him after the way of women. She saw his future and hers through glowing vistas of reform, and her first great deed was when she wrung from him his promise to cease fighting.

And he, after the way of men, pursuing the dream of love and striving for possession of the precious and deathless object of desire, had yielded. And yet, in the very moment of promising her, he knew vaguely, deep down, that he could never abandon the Game; that somewhere, sometime, in the future, he must go back to it. And he had had a swift vision of his mother and brothers and sisters, their multitudinous wants, the house with its painting and repairing, its street assessments and taxes, and of the coming of children to him and Genevieve, and of his own daily wage in the sail-making loft. But the next moment the vision was dismissed, as such warnings are always dismissed, and he saw before him only Genevieve, and he knew only his hunger for her and the call of his being to her; and he accepted calmly her calm assumption of his life and actions.

He was twenty, she was eighteen, boy and girl, the pair of them, and made for progeny, healthy and normal, with steady blood pounding through their bodies; and wherever they went together, even on Sunday outings across the bay amongst people who did not know him, eyes were continually drawn to them. He matched her girl's beauty with his boy's beauty, her grace with his strength, her delicacy of line and fibre with the harsher vigor and muscle of the male. Frank-faced, fresh-colored, almost ingenuous in expression, eyes blue and wide apart, he drew and held the gaze of more than one woman far above him in the social scale. Of such glances and dim maternal promptings he was quite unconscious, though Genevieve was quick to see and understand; and she knew each time the pang of a fierce joy in that he was hers and that she held him in the hollow of her hand. He did see, however, and rather resented, the men's glances drawn by her. These, too, she saw and understood as he did not dream of understanding.

CHAPTER III

Genevieve slipped on a pair of Joe's shoes, light-soled and dapper, and laughed with Lottie, who stooped to turn up the trousers for her. Lottie was his sister, and in the secret. To her was due the inveigling of his mother into making a neighborhood call so that they could have the house to themselves. They went down into the kitchen where Joe was waiting. His face brightened as he came to meet her, love shining frankly forth.

"Now get up those skirts, Lottie," he commanded. "Haven't any time to waste. There, that'll do. You see, you only want the bottoms of the pants to show. The coat will cover the rest. Now let's see how it'll fit.

"Borrowed it from Chris; he's a dead sporty sport—little, but oh, my!" he went on, helping Genevieve into an overcoat which fell to her heels and which fitted her as a tailor-made overcoat should fit the man for whom it is made.

Joe put a cap on her head and turned up the collar, which was generous to exaggeration, meeting the cap and completely hiding her hair. When he buttoned the collar in front, its points served to cover the cheeks, chin and mouth were buried in its depths, and a close scrutiny revealed only shadowy eyes and a little less shadowy nose. She walked across the room, the bottom of the trousers just showing as the bang of the coat was disturbed by movement.

"A sport with a cold and afraid of catching more, all right all right," the boy laughed, proudly surveying his handiwork. "How much money you got? I'm layin' ten to six. Will you take the short end?"

"Who's short?" she asked.

"Ponta, of course," Lottie blurted out her hurt, as though there could be any question of it even for an instant.

"Of course," Genevieve said sweetly, "only I don't know much about such things."

This time Lottie kept her lips together, but the new hurt showed on her face. Joe looked at his watch and said it was time to go. His sister's arms went about his neck, and she kissed him soundly on the lips. She kissed Genevieve, too, and saw them to the gate, one arm of her brother about her waist.

"What does ten to six mean?" Genevieve asked, the while their footfalls rang out on the frosty air.

"That I'm the long end, the favorite," he answered. "That a man bets ten dollars at the ring side that I win against six dollars another man is betting that I lose."

"But if you're the favorite and everybody thinks you'll win, how does anybody bet against you?"

"That's what makes prize-fighting—difference of opinion," he laughed. "Besides, there's always the chance of a lucky punch, an accident. Lots of chance," he said gravely.

She shrank against him, clingingly and protectingly, and he laughed with surety.

"You wait, and you'll see. An' don't get scared at the start. The first few rounds'll be something fierce. That's Ponta's strong point. He's a wild man, with an kinds of punches,—a whirlwind,—and he gets his man in the first rounds. He's put away a whole lot of cleverer and better men than him. It's up to me to live through it, that's all. Then he'll be all in. Then I go after him, just watch. You'll know when I go after him, an' I'll get'm, too."

They came to the hall, on a dark street-corner, ostensibly the quarters of an athletic club, but in reality an institution designed for pulling off fights and keeping within the police ordinance. Joe drew away from her, and they walked apart to the entrance.

"Keep your hands in your pockets whatever you do," Joe warned her, "and it'll be all right. Only a couple of minutes of it."

"He's with me," Joe said to the door-keeper, who was talking with a policeman.

Both men greeted him familiarly, taking no notice of his companion.

"They never tumbled; nobody'll tumble," Joe assured her, as they climbed the stairs to the second story. "And even if they did, they wouldn't know who it was and they's keep it mum for me. Here, come in here!"

He whisked her into a little office-like room and left her seated on a dusty, broken-bottomed chair. A few minutes later he was back again, clad in a long bath robe, canvas shoes on his feet. She began to tremble against him, and his arm passed gently around her.

"It'll be all right, Genevieve," he said encouragingly. "I've got it all fixed. Nobody'll tumble."

"It's you, Joe," she said. "I don't care for myself. It's you."

"Don't care for yourself! But that's what I thought you were afraid of!"

He looked at her in amazement, the wonder of woman bursting upon him in a more transcendent glory than ever, and he had seen much of the wonder of woman in Genevieve. He was speechless for a moment, and then stammered:—

"You mean me? And you don't care what people think? or anything?—or anything?"

A sharp double knock at the door, and a sharper "Get a move on yerself, Joe!" brought him back to immediate things.

"Quick, one last kiss, Genevieve," he whispered, almost holily. "It's my last fight, an' I'll fight as never before with you lookin' at me."

The next she knew, the pressure of his lips yet warm on hers, she was in a group of jostling young fellows, none of whom seemed to take the slightest notice of her. Several had their coats off and their shirt sleeves rolled up. They entered the hall from the rear, still keeping the casual formation of the group, and moved slowly up a side aisle.

It was a crowded, ill-lighted hall, barn-like in its proportions, and the smoke-laden air gave a peculiar distortion to everything. She felt as though she would stifle. There were shrill cries of boys selling programmes and soda water, and there was a great bass rumble of masculine voices. She heard a voice offering ten to six on Joe Fleming. The utterance was monotonous—hopeless, it seemed to her, and she felt a quick thrill. It was her Joe against whom everybody was to bet.

And she felt other thrills. Her blood was touched, as by fire, with romance, adventure—the unknown, the mysterious, the terrible—as she penetrated this haunt of men where women came not. And there were other thrills. It was the only time in her life she had dared the rash thing. For the first time she was overstepping the bounds laid down by that harshest of tyrants, the Mrs. Grundy of the working class. She felt fear, and for herself, though the moment before she had been thinking only of Joe.

Before she knew it, the front of the hall had been reached, and she had gone up half a dozen steps into a small dressing-room. This was crowded to suffocation—by men who played the Game, she concluded, in one capacity or another. And here she lost Joe. But before the real personal fright could soundly clutch her, one of the young fellows said gruffly, "Come along with me, you," and as she wedged out at his heels she noticed that another one of the escort was following her.

They came upon a sort of stage, which accommodated three rows of men; and she caught her first glimpse of the squared ring. She was on a level with it, and so near that she could have reached out and touched its ropes. She noticed that it was covered with padded canvas. Beyond the ring, and on either side, as in a fog, she could see the crowded house.

The dressing-room she had left abutted upon one corner of the ring. Squeezing her way after her guide through the seated men, she crossed the end of the hall and entered a similar dressing-room at the other corner of the ring.

"Now don't make a noise, and stay here till I come for you," instructed her guide, pointing out a peep-hole arrangement in the wall of the room.

CHAPTER IV

She hurried to the peep-hole, and found herself against the ring. She could see the whole of it, though part of the audience was shut off. The ring was well lighted by an overhead cluster of patent gas-burners. The front row of the men she had squeezed past, because of their paper and pencils, she decided to be reporters from the local papers up-town. One of them was chewing gum. Behind them, on the other two rows of seats, she could make out firemen from the near-by engine-house and several policemen in uniform. In the middle of the front row, flanked by the reporters, sat the young chief of police. She was startled by catching sight of Mr. Clausen on the opposite side of the ring. There he sat, austere, side-whiskered, pink and white, close up against the front of the ring. Several seats farther on, in the same front row, she discovered Silverstein, his weazen features glowing with anticipation.

A few cheers heralded the advent of several young fellows, in shirt-sleeves, carrying buckets, bottles, and towels, who crawled through the ropes and crossed to the diagonal corner from her. One of them sat down on a stool and leaned back against the ropes. She saw that he was bare-legged, with canvas shoes on his feet, and that his body was swathed in a heavy white sweater. In the meantime another group had occupied the corner directly against her. Louder cheers drew her attention to it, and she saw Joe seated on a stool still clad in the bath robe, his short chestnut curls within a yard of her eyes.

A young man, in a black suit, with a mop of hair and a preposterously tall starched collar, walked to the centre of the ring and held up his hand.

"Gentlemen will please stop smoking," he said.

His effort was applauded by groans and cat-calls, and she noticed with indignation that nobody stopped smoking. Mr. Clausen held a burning match in his fingers while the announcement was being made, and then calmly lighted his cigar. She felt that she hated him in that moment. How was her Joe to fight in such an atmosphere? She could scarcely breathe herself, and she was only sitting down.

The announcer came over to Joe. He stood up. His bath robe fell away from him, and he stepped forth to the centre of the ring, naked save for the low canvas shoes and a narrow hip-cloth of white. Genevieve's eyes dropped. She sat alone, with none to see, but her face was burning with shame at sight of the beautiful nakedness of her lover. But she looked again, guiltily, for the joy that was hers in beholding what she knew must be sinful to behold. The leap of something within her and the stir of her being toward him must be sinful. But it was delicious sin, and she did not deny her eyes. In vain Mrs. Grundy admonished her. The pagan in her, original sin, and all nature urged her on. The mothers of all the past were whispering through her, and there was a clamour of the children unborn. But of this she knew nothing. She knew only that it was sin, and she lifted her head proudly, recklessly resolved, in one great surge of revolt, to sin to the uttermost.

She had never dreamed of the form under the clothes. The form, beyond the hands and the face, had no part in her mental processes. A child of garmented civilization, the garment was to her the form. The race of men was to her a race of garmented bipeds, with hands and faces and hair-covered heads. When she thought of Joe, the Joe instantly visualized on her mind was a clothed Joe—girl-cheeked, blue-eyed, curly-headed, but clothed. And there he stood, all but naked, godlike, in a white blaze of light. She had never conceived of the form of God except as nebulously naked, and the thought-association was startling. It seemed to her that her sin partook of sacrilege or blasphemy.

Her chromo-trained æsthetic sense exceeded its education and told her that here were beauty and wonder. She had always liked the physical presentment of Joe, but it was a presentment of clothes, and she had thought the pleasingness of it due to the neatness and taste with which he dressed. She had never dreamed that this lurked beneath. It dazzled her. His skin was fair as a woman's, far more satiny, and no rudimentary hair-growth marred its white lustre. This she perceived, but all the rest, the perfection of line and strength and development, gave pleasure without her knowing why. There was a cleanness and grace about it. His face was like a cameo, and his lips, parted in a smile, made it very boyish.

He smiled as he faced the audience, when the announcer, placing a hand on his shoulder, said: "Joe Fleming, the Pride of West Oakland."

Cheers and hand-clappings stormed up, and she heard affectionate cries of "Oh, you, Joe!" Men shouted it at him again and again.

He walked back to his corner. Never to her did he seem less a fighter than then. His eyes were too mild; there was not a spark of the beast in them, nor in his face, while his body seemed too fragile, what of its fairness and smoothness, and his face too boyish and sweet-tempered and intelligent. She did not have the expert's eye for the depth of chest, the wide nostrils, the recuperative lungs, and the muscles under their satin sheaths—crypts of energy wherein lurked the chemistry of destruction. To her he looked like a something of Dresden china, to be handled gently and with care, liable to be shattered to fragments by the first rough touch.

John Ponta, stripped of his white sweater by the pulling and hauling of two of his seconds, came to the centre of the ring. She knew terror as she looked at him. Here was the fighter—the beast with a streak for a forehead, with beady eyes under lowering and bushy brows, flat-nosed, thick-lipped, sullen-mouthed. He was heavy-jawed, bull-necked, and the short, straight hair of the head seemed to her frightened eyes the stiff bristles on a hog's back. Here were coarseness and brutishness—a thing savage, primordial, ferocious. He was swarthy to blackness, and his body was covered with a hairy growth that matted like a dog's on his chest and shoulders. He was deep-chested, thick-legged, large-muscled, but unshapely. His muscles were knots, and he was gnarled and knobby, twisted out of beauty by excess of strength.

"John Ponta, West Bay Athletic Club," said the announcer.

A much smaller volume of cheers greeted him. It was evident that the crowd favored Joe with its sympathy.

"Go in an' eat 'm, Ponta! Eat 'm up!" a voice shouted in the lull.

This was received by scornful cries and groans. He did not like it, for his sullen mouth twisted into a half-snarl as he went back to his corner. He was too decided an atavism to draw the crowd's admiration. Instinctively the crowd disliked him. He was an animal, lacking in intelligence and spirit, a menace and a thing of fear, as the tiger and the snake are menaces and things of fear, better behind the bars of a cage than running free in the open.

And he felt that the crowd had no relish for him. He was like an animal in the circle of its enemies, and he turned and glared at them with malignant eyes. Little Silverstein, shouting out Joe's name with high glee, shrank away from Ponta's gaze, shrivelled as in fierce heat, the sound gurgling and dying in his throat. Genevieve saw the little by-play, and as Ponta's eyes slowly swept round the circle of their hate and met hers, she, too, shrivelled and shrank back. The next moment they were past, pausing to centre long on Joe. It seemed to her that Ponta was working himself into a rage. Joe returned the gaze with mild boy's eyes, but his face grew serious.

The announcer escorted a third man to the centre of the ring, a genial-faced young fellow in shirt-sleeves.

"Eddy Jones, who will referee this contest," said the announcer.

"Oh, you, Eddy!" men shouted in the midst of the applause, and it was apparent to Genevieve that he, too, was well beloved.

Both men were being helped into the gloves by their seconds, and one of Ponta's seconds came over and examined the gloves before they went on Joe's hands. The referee called them to the centre of the ring. The seconds followed, and they made quite a group, Joe and Ponta facing each other, the referee in the middle, the seconds leaning with hands on one another's shoulders, their heads craned forward. The referee was talking, and all listened attentively.

The group broke up. Again the announcer came to the front.

"Joe Fleming fights at one hundred and twenty-eight," he said; "John Ponta at one hundred and forty. They will fight as long as one hand is free, and take care of themselves in the breakaway. The audience must remember that a decision must be given. There are no draws fought before this club."

He crawled through the ropes and dropped from the ring to the floor. There was a scuttling in the corners as the seconds cleared out through the ropes, taking with them the stools and buckets. Only remained in the ring the two fighters and the referee. A gong sounded. The two men advanced rapidly to the centre. Their right hands extended and for a fraction of an instant met in a perfunctory shake. Then Ponta lashed out, savagely, right and left, and Joe escaped by springing back. Like a projectile, Ponta hurled himself after him and upon him.

The fight was on. Genevieve clutched one hand to her breast and watched. She was bewildered by the swiftness and savagery of Ponta's assault, and by the multitude of blows he struck. She felt that Joe was surely being destroyed. At times she could not see his face, so obscured was it by the flying gloves. But she could hear the resounding blows, and with the sound of each blow she felt a sickening sensation in the pit of her stomach. She did not know that what she heard was the impact of glove on glove, or glove on shoulder, and that no damage was being done.

She was suddenly aware that a change had come over the fight. Both men were clutching each other in a tense embrace; no blows were being struck at all. She recognized it to be what Joe had described to her as the "clinch." Ponta was struggling to free himself, Joe was holding on.

The referee shouted, "Break!" Joe made an effort to get away, but Ponta got one hand free and Joe rushed back into a second clinch, to escape the blow. But this time, she noticed, the heel of his glove was pressed against Ponta's mouth and chin, and at the second "Break!" of the referee, Joe shoved his opponent's head back and sprang clear himself.

For a brief several seconds she had an unobstructed view of her lover. Left foot a trifle advanced, knees slightly bent, he was crouching, with his head drawn well down between his shoulders and shielded by them. His hands were in position before him, ready either to attack or defend. The muscles of his body were tense, and as he moved about she could see them bunch up and writhe and crawl like live things under the white skin.

But again Ponta was upon him and he was struggling to live. He crouched a bit more, drew his body more compactly together, and covered up with his hands, elbows, and forearms. Blows rained upon him, and it looked to her as though he were being beaten to death.

But he was receiving the blows on his gloves and shoulders, rocking back and forth to the force of them like a tree in a storm, while the house cheered its delight. It was not until she understood this applause, and saw Silverstein half out of his seat and intensely, madly happy, and heard the "Oh, you, Joe's!" from many throats, that she realized that instead of being cruelly punished he was acquitting himself well. Then he would emerge for a moment, again to be enveloped and hidden in the whirlwind of Ponta's ferocity.

CHAPTER V

The gong sounded. It seemed they had been fighting half an hour, though from what Joe had told her she knew it had been only three minutes. With the crash of the gong Joe's seconds were through the ropes and running him into his corner for the blessed minute of rest. One man, squatting on the floor between his outstretched feet and elevating them by resting them on his knees, was violently chafing his legs. Joe sat on the stool, leaning far back into the corner, head thrown back and arms outstretched on the ropes to give easy expansion to the chest. With wide-open mouth he was breathing the towel-driven air furnished by two of the seconds, while listening to the counsel of still another second who talked with low voice in his ear and at the same time sponged off his face, shoulders, and chest.

Hardly had all this been accomplished (it had taken no more than several seconds), when the gong sounded, the seconds scuttled through the ropes with their paraphernalia, and Joe and Ponta were advancing against each other to the centre of the ring. Genevieve had no idea that a minute could be so short. For a moment she felt that this rest had been cut, and was suspicious of she knew not what.

Ponta lashed out, right and left, savagely as ever, and though Joe blocked the blows, such was the force of them that he was knocked backward several steps. Ponta was after him with the spring of a tiger. In the involuntary effort to maintain equilibrium, Joe had uncovered himself, flinging one arm out and lifting his head from beneath the sheltering shoulders. So swiftly had Ponta followed him, that a terrible swinging blow was coming at his unguarded jaw. He ducked forward and down, Ponta's fist just missing the back of his head. As he came back to the perpendicular, Ponta's left fist drove at him in a straight punch that would have knocked him backward through the ropes. Again, and with a swiftness an inappreciable fraction of time quicker than Ponta's, he ducked forward. Ponta's fist grazed the backward slope of the shoulder, and glanced off into the air. Ponta's right drove straight out, and the graze was repeated as Joe ducked into the safety of a clinch.

Genevieve sighed with relief, her tense body relaxing and a faintness coming over her. The crowd was cheering madly. Silverstein was on his feet, shouting, gesticulating, completely out of himself. And even Mr. Clausen was yelling his enthusiasm, at the top of his lungs, into the ear of his nearest neighbor.

The clinch was broken and the fight went on. Joe blocked, and backed, and slid around the ring, avoiding blows and living somehow through the whirlwind onslaughts. Rarely did he strike blows himself, for Ponta had a quick eye and could defend as well as attack, while Joe had no chance against the other's enormous vitality. His hope lay in that Ponta himself should ultimately consume his strength.

But Genevieve was beginning to wonder why her lover did not fight. She grew angry. She wanted to see him wreak vengeance on this beast that had persecuted him so. Even as she waxed impatient, the chance came, and Joe whipped his fist to Ponta's mouth. It was a staggering blow. She saw Ponta's head go back with a jerk and the quick dye of blood upon his lips. The blow, and the great shout from the audience, angered him. He rushed like a wild man. The fury of his previous assaults was as nothing compared with the fury of this one. And there was no more opportunity for another blow. Joe was too busy living through the storm he had already caused, blocking, covering up, and ducking into the safety and respite of the clinches.

But the clinch was not all safety and respite. Every instant of it was intense watchfulness, while the breakaway was still more dangerous. Genevieve had noticed, with a slight touch of amusement, the curious way in which Joe snuggled his body in against Ponta's in the clinches; but she had not realized why, until, in one such clinch, before the snuggling in could be effected, Ponta's fist whipped straight up in the air from under, and missed Joe's chin by a hair's-breadth. In another and later clinch, when she had already relaxed and sighed her relief at seeing him safely snuggled, Ponta, his chin over Joe's shoulder, lifted his right arm and struck a terrible downward blow on the small of the back. The crowd groaned its apprehension, while Joe quickly locked his opponent's arms to prevent a repetition of the blow.

The gong struck, and after the fleeting minute of rest, they went at it again—in Joe's corner, for Ponta had made a rush to meet him clear across the ring. Where the blow had been over the kidneys, the white skin had become bright red. This splash of color, the size of the glove, fascinated and frightened Genevieve so that she could scarcely take her eyes from it. Promptly, in the next clinch, the blow was repeated; but after that Joe usually managed to give Ponta the heel of the glove on the mouth and so hold his head back. This prevented the striking of the blow; but three times more, before the round ended, Ponta effected the trick, each time striking the same vulnerable part.

Another rest and another round went by, with no further damage to Joe and no diminution of strength on the part of Ponta. But in the beginning of the fifth round, Joe, caught in a corner, made as though to duck into a clinch. Just before it was effected, and at the precise moment that Ponta was ready with his own body to receive the snuggling in of Joe's body, Joe drew back slightly and drove with his fists at his opponent's unprotected stomach. Lightning-like blows they were, four of them, right and left; and heavy they were, for Ponta winced away from them and staggered back, half dropping his arms, his shoulders drooping forward and in, as though he were about to double in at the waist and collapse. Joe's quick eye saw the opening, and he smashed straight out upon Ponta's mouth, following instantly with a half swing, half hook, for the jaw. It missed, striking the cheek instead, and sending Ponta staggering sideways.

The house was on its feet, shouting, to a man. Genevieve could hear men crying, "He's got 'm, he's got 'm!" and it seemed to her the beginning of the end. She, too, was out of herself; softness and tenderness had vanished; she exulted with each crushing blow her lover delivered.

But Ponta's vitality was yet to be reckoned with. As, like a tiger, he had followed Joe up, Joe now followed him up. He made another half swing, half hook, for Ponta's jaw, and Ponta, already recovering his wits and strength, ducked cleanly. Joe's fist passed on through empty air, and so great was the momentum of the blow that it carried him around, in a half twirl, sideways. Then Ponta lashed out with his left. His glove landed on Joe's unguarded neck. Genevieve saw her lover's arms drop to his sides as his body lifted, went backward, and fell limply to the floor. The referee, bending over him, began to count the seconds, emphasizing the passage of each second with a downward sweep of his right arm.

The audience was still as death. Ponta had partly turned to the house to receive the approval that was his due, only to be met by this chill, graveyard silence. Quick wrath surged up in him. It was unfair. His opponent only was applauded—if he struck a blow, if he escaped a blow; he, Ponta, who had forced the fighting from the start, had received no word of cheer.

His eyes blazed as he gathered himself together and sprang to his prostrate foe. He crouched alongside of him, right arm drawn back and ready for a smashing blow the instant Joe should start to rise. The referee, still bending over and counting with his right hand, shoved Ponta back with his left. The latter, crouching, circled around, and the referee circled with him, thrusting him back and keeping between him and the fallen man.

"Four—five—six—" the count went on, and Joe, rolling over on his face, squirmed weakly to draw himself to his knees. This he succeeded in doing, resting on one knee, a hand to the floor on either side and the other leg bent under him to help him rise. "Take the count! Take the count!" a dozen voices rang out from the audience.

"For God's sake, take the count!" one of Joe's seconds cried warningly from the edge of the ring. Genevieve gave him one swift glance, and saw the young fellow's face, drawn and white, his lips unconsciously moving as he kept the count with the referee.

"Seven—eight—nine—" the seconds went.

The ninth sounded and was gone, when the referee gave Ponta a last backward shove and Joe came to his feet, bunched up, covered up, weak, but cool, very cool. Ponta hurled himself upon him with terrific force, delivering an uppercut and a straight punch. But Joe blocked the two, ducked a third, stepped to the side to avoid a fourth, and was then driven backward into a corner by a hurricane of blows. He was exceedingly weak. He tottered as he kept his footing, and staggered back and forth. His back was against the ropes. There was no further retreat. Ponta paused, as if to make doubly sure, then feinted with his left and struck fiercely with his right with all his strength. But Joe ducked into a clinch and was for a moment saved.

Ponta struggled frantically to free himself. He wanted to give the finish to this foe already so far gone. But Joe was holding on for life, resisting the other's every effort, as fast as one hold or grip was torn loose finding a new one by which to cling. "Break!" the referee commanded. Joe held on tighter. "Make 'm break! Why the hell don't you make 'm break?" Ponta panted at the referee. Again the latter commanded the break. Joe refused, keeping, as he well knew, within his rights. Each moment of the clinch his strength was coming back to him, his brain was clearing, the cobwebs were disappearing from before his eyes. The round was young, and he must live, somehow, through the nearly three minutes of it yet to run.

The referee clutched each by the shoulder and sundered them violently, passing quickly between them as he thrust them backward in order to make a clean break of it. The moment he was free, Ponta sprang at Joe like a wild animal bearing down its prey. But Joe covered up, blocked, and fell into a clinch. Again Ponta struggled to get free, Joe held on, and the referee thrust them apart. And again Joe avoided damage and clinched.

Genevieve realized that in the clinches he was not being beaten—why, then, did not the referee let him hold on? It was cruel. She hated the genial-faced Eddy Jones in those moments, and she partly rose from her chair, her hands clenched with anger, the nails cutting into the palms till they hurt. The rest of the round, the three long minutes of it, was a succession of clinches and breaks. Not once did Ponta succeed in striking his opponent the deadly final blow. And Ponta was like a madman, raging because of his impotency in the face of his helpless and all but vanquished foe. One blow, only one blow, and he could not deliver it! Joe's ring experience and coolness saved him. With shaken consciousness and trembling body, he clutched and held on, while the ebbing life turned and flooded up in him again. Once, in his passion, unable to hit him, Ponta made as though to lift him up and hurl him to the floor.

"V'y don't you bite him?" Silverstein taunted shrilly.

In the stillness the sally was heard over the whole house, and the audience, relieved of its anxiety for its favorite, laughed with an uproariousness that had in it the note of hysteria. Even Genevieve felt that there was something irresistibly funny in the remark, and the relief of the audience was communicated to her; yet she felt sick and faint, and was overwrought with horror at what she had seen and was seeing.

"Bite 'm! Bite 'm!" voices from the recovered audience were shouting. "Chew his ear off, Ponta! That's the only way you can get 'm! Eat 'm up! Eat 'm up! Oh, why don't you eat 'm up?"

The effect was bad on Ponta. He became more frenzied than ever, and more impotent. He panted and sobbed, wasting his effort by too much effort, losing sanity and control and futilely trying to compensate for the loss by excess of physical endeavor. He knew only the blind desire to destroy, shook Joe in the clinches as a terrier might a rat, strained and struggled for freedom of body and arms, and all the while Joe calmly clutched and held on. The referee worked manfully and fairly to separate them. Perspiration ran down his face. It took all his strength to split those clinging bodies, and no sooner had he split them than Joe fell unharmed into another embrace and the work had to be done all over again. In vain, when freed, did Ponta try to avoid the clutching arms and twining body. He could not keep away. He had to come close in order to strike, and each time Joe baffled him and caught him in his arms.

And Genevieve, crouched in the little dressing-room and peering through the peep-hole, was baffled, too. She was an interested party in what seemed a death-struggle—was not one of the fighters her Joe?—but the audience understood and she did not. The Game had not unveiled to her. The lure of it was beyond her. It was greater mystery than ever. She could not comprehend its power. What delight could there be for Joe in that brutal surging and straining of bodies, those fierce clutches, fiercer blows, and terrible hurts? Surely, she, Genevieve, offered more than that—rest, and content, and sweet, calm joy. Her bid for the heart of him and the soul of him was finer and more generous than the bid of the Game; yet he dallied with both—held her in his arms, but turned his head to listen to that other and siren call she could not understand.

The gong struck. The round ended with a break in Ponta's corner. The white-faced young second was through the ropes with the first clash of sound. He seized Joe in his arms, lifted him clear of the floor, and ran with him across the ring to his own corner. His seconds worked over him furiously, chafing his legs, slapping his abdomen, stretching the hip-cloth out with their fingers so that he might breathe more easily. For the first time Genevieve saw the stomach-breathing of a man, an abdomen that rose and fell far more with every breath than her breast rose and fell after she had run for a car. The pungency of ammonia bit her nostrils, wafted to her from the soaked sponge wherefrom he breathed the fiery fumes that cleared his brain. He gargled his mouth and throat, took a suck at a divided lemon, and all the while the towels worked like mad, driving oxygen into his lungs to purge the pounding blood and send it back revivified for the struggle yet to come. His heated body was sponged with water, doused with it, and bottles were turned mouth-downward on his head.

CHAPTER VI

The gong for the sixth round struck, and both men advanced to meet each other, their bodies glistening with water. Ponta rushed two-thirds of the way across the ring, so intent was he on getting at his man before full recovery could be effected. But Joe had lived through. He was strong again, and getting stronger. He blocked several vicious blows and then smashed back, sending Ponta reeling. He attempted to follow up, but wisely forbore and contented himself with blocking and covering up in the whirlwind his blow had raised.

The fight was as it had been at the beginning—Joe protecting, Ponta rushing. But Ponta was never at ease. He did not have it all his own way. At any moment, in his fiercest onslaughts, his opponent was liable to lash out and reach him. Joe saved his strength. He struck one blow to Ponta's ten, but his one blow rarely missed. Ponta overwhelmed him in the attacks, yet could do nothing with him, while Joe's tiger-like strokes, always imminent, compelled respect. They toned Ponta's ferocity. He was no longer able to go in with the complete abandon of destructiveness which had marked his earlier efforts.

But a change was coming over the fight. The audience was quick to note it, and even Genevieve saw it by the beginning of the ninth round. Joe was taking the offensive. In the clinches it was he who brought his fist down on the small of the back, striking the terrible kidney blow. He did it once, in each clinch, but with all his strength, and he did it every clinch. Then, in the breakaways, he began to uppercut Ponta on the stomach, or to hook his jaw or strike straight out upon the mouth. But at first sign of a coming of a whirlwind, Joe would dance nimbly away and cover up.

Two rounds of this went by, and three, but Ponta's strength, though perceptibly less, did not diminish rapidly. Joe's task was to wear down that strength, not with one blow, nor ten, but with blow after blow, without end, until that enormous strength should be beaten sheer out of its body. There was no rest for the man. Joe followed him up, step by step, his advancing left foot making an audible tap, tap, tap, on the hard canvas. Then there would come a sudden leap in, tiger-like, a blow struck, or blows, and a swift leap back, whereupon the left foot would take up again its tapping advance. When Ponta made his savage rushes, Joe carefully covered up, only to emerge, his left foot going tap, tap, tap, as he immediately followed up.

Ponta was slowly weakening. To the crowd the end was a foregone conclusion.

"Oh, you, Joe!" it yelled its admiration and affection.

"It's a shame to take the money!" it mocked. "Why don't you eat 'm, Ponta? Go on in an' eat 'm!"

In the one-minute intermissions Ponta's seconds worked over him as they had not worked before. Their calm trust in his tremendous vitality had been betrayed. Genevieve watched their excited efforts, while she listened to the white-faced second cautioning Joe.

"Take your time," he was saying. "You've got 'm, but you got to take your time. I've seen 'm fight. He's got a punch to the end of the count. I've seen 'm knocked out and clean batty, an' go on punching just the same. Mickey Sullivan had 'm goin'. Puts 'm to the mat as fast as he crawls up, six times, an' then leaves an opening. Ponta reaches for his jaw, an two minutes afterward Mickey's openin' his eyes an' askin' what's doin'. So you've got to watch 'm. No goin' in an' absorbin' one of them lucky punches, now. I got money on this fight, but I don't call it mine till he's counted out."

Ponta was being doused with water. As the gong sounded, one of his seconds inverted a water bottle on his head. He started toward the centre of the ring, and the second followed him for several steps, keeping the bottle still inverted. The referee shouted at him, and he fled the ring, dropping the bottle as he fled. It rolled over and over, the water gurgling out upon the canvas till the referee, with a quick flirt of his toe, sent the bottle rolling through the ropes.

In all the previous rounds Genevieve had not seen Joe's fighting face which had been prefigured to her that morning in the department store. Sometimes his face had been quite boyish; other times, when taking his fiercest punishment, it had been bleak and gray; and still later, when living through and clutching and holding on, it had taken on a wistful expression. But now, out of danger himself and as he forced the fight, his fighting face came upon him. She saw it and shuddered. It removed him so far from her. She had thought she knew him, all of him, and held him in the hollow of her hand; but this she did not know—this face of steel, this mouth of steel, these eyes of steel flashing the light and glitter of steel. It seemed to her the passionless face of an avenging angel, stamped only with the purpose of the Lord.

Ponta attempted one of his old-time rushes, but was stopped on the mouth. Implacable, insistent, ever menacing, never letting him rest, Joe followed him up. The round, the thirteenth, closed with a rush, in Ponta's corner. He attempted a rally, was brought to his knees, took the nine seconds' count, and then tried to clinch into safety, only to receive four of Joe's terrible stomach punches, so that with the gong he fell back, gasping, into the arms of his seconds.

Joe ran across the ring to his own corner.

"Now I'm going to get 'm," he said to his second.

"You sure fixed 'm that time," the latter answered. "Nothin' to stop you now but a lucky punch. Watch out for it."

Joe leaned forward, feet gathered under him for a spring, like a foot-racer waiting the start. He was waiting for the gong. When it sounded he shot forward and across the ring, catching Ponta in the midst of his seconds as he rose from his stool. And in the midst of his seconds he went down, knocked down by a right-hand blow. As he arose from the confusion of buckets, stools, and seconds, Joe put him down again. And yet a third time he went down before he could escape from his own corner.

Joe had at last become the whirlwind. Genevieve remembered his "just watch, you'll know when I go after him." The house knew it, too. It was on its feet, every voice raised in a fierce yell. It was the blood-cry of the crowd, and it sounded to her like what she imagined must be the howling of wolves. And what with confidence in her lover's victory she found room in her heart to pity Ponta.

In vain he struggled to defend himself, to block, to cover up, to duck, to clinch into a moment's safety. That moment was denied him. Knockdown after knockdown was his portion. He was knocked to the canvas backwards, and sideways, was punched in the clinches and in the breakaways—stiff, jolty blows that dazed his brain and drove the strength from his muscles. He was knocked into the corners and out again, against the ropes, rebounding, and with another blow against the ropes once more. He fanned the air with his arms, showering savage blows upon emptiness. There was nothing human left in him. He was the beast incarnate, roaring and raging and being destroyed. He was smashed down to his knees, but refused to take the count, staggering to his feet only to be met stiff-handed on the mouth and sent hurling back against the ropes.

In sore travail, gasping, reeling, panting, with glazing eyes and sobbing breath, grotesque and heroic, fighting to the last, striving to get at his antagonist, he surged and was driven about the ring. And in that moment Joe's foot slipped on the wet canvas. Ponta's swimming eyes saw and knew the chance. All the fleeing strength of his body gathered itself together for the lightning lucky punch. Even as Joe slipped the other smote him, fairly on the point of the chin. He went over backward. Genevieve saw his muscles relax while he was yet in the air, and she heard the thud of his head on the canvas.

The noise of the yelling house died suddenly. The referee, stooping over the inert body, was counting the seconds. Ponta tottered and fell to his knees. He struggled to his feet, swaying back and forth as he tried to sweep the audience with his hatred. His legs were trembling and bending under him; he was choking and sobbing, fighting to breathe. He reeled backward, and saved himself from falling by a blind clutching for the ropes. He clung there, drooping and bending and giving in all his body, his head upon his chest, until the referee counted the fatal tenth second and pointed to him in token that he had won.

He received no applause, and he squirmed through the ropes,

snakelike, into the arms of his seconds, who helped him to the floor and supported him down the aisle into the crowd. Joe remained where he had fallen. His seconds carried him into his corner and placed him on the stool. Men began climbing into the ring, curious to see, but were roughly shoved out by the policemen, who were already there.

Genevieve looked on from her peep-hole. She was not greatly perturbed. Her lover had been knocked out. In so far as disappointment was his, she shared it with him; but that was all. She even felt glad in a way. The Game had played him false, and he was more surely hers. She had heard of knockouts from him. It often took men some time to recover from the effects. It was not till she heard the seconds asking for the doctor that she felt really worried.

They passed his limp body through the ropes to the stage, and it disappeared beyond the limits of her peep-hole. Then the door of her dressing-room was thrust open and a number of men came in. They were carrying Joe. He was laid down on the dusty floor, his head resting on the knee of one of the seconds. No one seemed surprised by her presence. She came over and knelt beside him. His eyes were closed, his lips slightly parted. His wet hair was plastered in straight locks about his face. She lifted one of his hands. It was very heavy, and the lifelessness of it shocked her. She looked suddenly at the faces of the seconds and of the men about her. They seemed frightened, all save one, and he was cursing, in a low voice, horribly. She looked up and saw Silverstein standing beside her. He, too, seemed frightened. He rested a kindly hand on her shoulder, tightening the fingers with a sympathetic pressure.

This sympathy frightened her. She began to feel dazed. There was a bustle as somebody entered the room. The person came forward, proclaiming irritably: "Get out! Get out! You've got to clear the room!"

A number of men silently obeyed.

"Who are you?" he abruptly demanded of Genevieve. "A girl, as I'm alive!"

"That's all right, she's his girl," spoke up a young fellow she recognized as her guide.

"And you?" the other man blurted explosively at Silverstein.

"I'm vit her," he answered truculently.

"She works for him," explained the young fellow. "It's all right, I tell you."

The newcomer grunted and knelt down. He passed a hand over the damp head, grunted again, and arose to his feet.

"This is no case for me," he said. "Send for the ambulance."

Then the thing became a dream to Genevieve. Maybe she had fainted, she did not know, but for what other reason should Silverstein have his arm around her supporting her? All the faces seemed blurred and unreal. Fragments of a discussion came to her ears. The young fellow who had been her guide was saying something about reporters. "You vill get your name in der papers," she could hear Silverstein saying to her, as from a great distance; and she knew she was shaking her head in refusal.

There was an eruption of new faces, and she saw Joe carried out on a canvas stretcher. Silverstein was buttoning the long overcoat and drawing the collar about her face. She felt the night air on her cheek, and looking up saw the clear, cold stars. She jammed into a seat. Silverstein was beside her. Joe was there, too, still on his stretcher, with blankets over his naked body; and there was a man in blue uniform who spoke kindly to her, though she did not know what he said. Horses' hoofs were clattering, and she was lurching somewhere through the night.

Next, light and voices, and a smell of iodoform. This must be the receiving hospital, she thought, this the operating table, those the doctors. They were examining Joe. One of them, a dark-eyed, dark-bearded, foreign-looking man, rose up from bending over the table.

"Never saw anything like it," he was saying to another man. "The whole back of the skull."

Her lips were hot and dry, and there was an intolerable ache in her throat. But why didn't she cry? She ought to cry; she felt it incumbent upon her. There was Lottie (there had been another change in the dream), across the little narrow cot from her, and she was crying. Somebody was saying something about the coma of death. It was not the foreign-looking doctor, but somebody else. It did not matter who it was. What time was it? As if in answer, she saw the faint white light of dawn on the windows.

"I was going to be married to-day," she said to Lottie.

And from across the cot his sister wailed, "Don't, don't!" and, covering her face, sobbed afresh.

This, then, was the end of it all—of the carpets, and furniture, and the little rented house; of the meetings and walking out, the thrilling nights of starshine, the deliciousness of surrender, the loving and the being loved. She was stunned by the awful facts of this Game she did not understand—the grip it laid on men's souls, its irony and faithlessness, its risks and hazards and fierce insurgences of the blood, making woman pitiful, not the be-all and end-all of man, but his toy and his pastime; to woman his mothering and caretaking, his moods and his moments, but to the Game his days and nights of striving, the tribute of his head and hand, his most patient toil and wildest effort, all the strain and the stress of his being—to the Game, his heart's desire.

Silverstein was helping her to her feet. She obeyed blindly, the daze of the dream still on her. His hand grasped her arm and he was turning her toward the door.

"Oh, why don't you kiss him?" Lottie cried out, her dark eyes mournful and passionate.

Genevieve stooped obediently over the quiet clay and pressed her lips to the lips yet warm. The door opened and she passed into another room. There stood Mrs. Silverstein, with angry eyes that snapped vindictively at sight of her boy's clothes.

Silverstein looked beseechingly at his spouse, but she burst forth savagely:—

"Vot did I tell you, eh? Vot did I tell you? You vood haf a bruiser for your steady! An' now your name vill be in all der papers! At a prize fight—vit boy's clothes on! You liddle strumpet! You hussy! You—"

But a flood of tears welled into her eyes and voice, and with her fat arms outstretched, ungainly, ludicrous, holy with motherhood, she tottered over to the quiet girl and folded her to her breast. She muttered gasping, inarticulate love-words, rocking slowly to and fro the while, and patting Genevieve's shoulder with her ponderous hand.

www.ingramcontent.com/pod-product-compliance
Lightning Source LLC
Chambersburg PA
CBHW011516170626
46810CB00009B/3392
9781647994266